TWISTED PATH

A BODHI KING NOVEL

MELISSA F. MILLER

BROWN STREET BOOKS

ALSO BY MELISSA F. MILLER

Chilling Effect

Calculated Risk

Called Home

The Bodhi King Novels

Dark Path

Lonely Path

Hidden Path

Twisted Path

The We Sisters Three Romantic Comedic Mysteries

Rosemary's Gravy

Sage of Innocence

Thyme to Live

Lost and Gowned

Wedding Bells and Hoodoo Spells

CHAPTER ONE

I n Japanese and Chinese mythology, the kirin or qilin is a chimerical single-horned, bearded, sometimes-winged creature with the body of a deer, the hooves of a horse, and the tail of an ox. Often compared to the dragon or unicorn of Western mythology, the beast is commonly found in Buddhist iconography.

Buddhist sources depict the creature as so gentle and peaceful that it walks on clouds so as not to harm even a blade of grass. Taoist folklore, however, casts this chimera as a divine judge of good and wickedness. Human judges were said to rely on the creature to determine guilt or innocence in difficult court cases. The qilin would use its horn to gore a guilty party to death.

November 29, 2012

D amon Tenley stared down at the lifeless body, his hands hanging limply by his sides. The paperweight, slick with blood and brain matter, slipped from his grasp and hit the hardwood floor with a loud thud. He flinched at the sound and, instinctively, looked to the woman on the bed for her reaction.

He instantly realized his mistake and snorted. *She's dead, you idiot.*

The bedroom was overheated, steam rising from the hissing radiators, and sweat beaded on his forehead. But Damon shook. He was cold. Freezing, actually.

You're going into shock, some remote part of his brain informed him. *You need to get out of here, fast.*

He staggered across the room to the bathroom and lurched through the open door. He barreled into the vanity, his hip bone connecting with the corner, but the pain didn't register. He gripped the cold water faucet and turned it on, full blast. He cupped his trembling hands under the stream of water to catch it. Then he splashed his face, rinsed his mouth, and spit into the bowl. He inhaled deeply, trying to slow his rapid heartbeat.

He hadn't expected to feel anything. He'd grown up

hunting. Done two tours in Afghanistan. Buried both his parents. He was no stranger to death.

But he hadn't killed a deer. Or an insurgent. The body on the bed didn't belong to a cancer-ravaged senior citizen who chose hospice over another round of toxic cocktails. It belonged to an innocent. She was vibrant and young and stunningly gorgeous. Or at least, she had been. Now, with her dented skull caved into her bloodied, slack face, she was gruesome.

His eyes flicked toward the bedroom. There was no time for this. The husband could be on his way home right now.

He grabbed one of the festive red-and-green plaid hand towels from the rack on the wall and patted his face dry. Then he wiped down the sink basin, the faucet, and the light switch.

He stuffed the towel into his pocket and hurried through the bedroom toward the hallway, averting his eyes from the dead woman on the bed. Her husband was at a department holiday party. He shouldn't be home for hours; but Damon had to get out of the house *now*. Before he lost it.

He hurled himself down the wide, walnut staircase, skidded to a stop at the bottom, rounded the corner, and ran down the hallway to the kitchen and the stairs leading to the cellar.

He plunged down into the dark, earthen basement, not bothering to pull the chain to turn on the exposed bulb. Even in the growing darkness, he knew he could find his way to the casement window he'd smashed to gain entry.

The blustery wind howled through the broken window, calling to him, guiding him toward his way out.

He crunched over the scattered shards of glass and hoisted himself up onto the metal utility sink. Then he shuffled along the edge like a tightrope walker until he reached the rough wall directly below the window.

He curled his fingers around the bottom lip of the window frame and scrabbled up, his feet swinging wildly. He maneuvered onto his stomach and eased through the opening, ignoring the sting of pain when his right cheek grazed the jagged glass shards that stubbornly clung to the pane.

He rolled out into the window well and crouched on the cold cement long enough to catch his breath.

Then he ducked low and crept through the small backyard. Once he reached the cover of the trees, he stood upright and darted to the short back fence. He vaulted it easily and melted into the dark alleyway's shadows.

His heart thudded in his ears. He'd done it. He'd

gotten rid of Raina Noor, like he promised he would. He'd earned his twenty thousand, and then some. Hell, there might even be a bonus in it for him.

But that wasn't why he did it. It wasn't about the money. Not at all.

CHAPTER TWO

The present day

"It was a paid hit. Damon Tenley murdered Raina Noor in exchange for twenty thousand dollars cash," Detective Burton Gilbert rumbled. His deep bass voice filled the hushed room as he explained the history to the inquisitive uniformed officer at his side.

Officer Meredith Vitanni stared down at the corpse sprawled across the bed. "And Noor was married to this guy?"

"Right. This poor SOB is Giles Noor. Killed in the

same house, in what looks to be the same bed, by the same apparent method. Six years ago, Tenley bashed his wife's head in right here in this room."

"Damn," Vitanni breathed. "What are the odds?"

Was she serious?

"I doubt it's a coincidence, Officer."

A bright red stain spread up her neck and across her cheeks. "I ... wait ... you think Tenley did this?"

"How in the hell would Tenley have killed Giles Noor?" an amused voice said from the doorway.

Burton knew before he turned who he'd find standing on the threshold. Detective Chrysanthemum Martin, the only other person on the homicide squad who'd been in the department when Raina Noor was murdered. Chrys had been the first to respond to the original Noor murder. She'd been comforting a sobbing Giles Noor when Burton had arrived.

Now she arched one groomed eyebrow at him, as if to ask where the department had found Vitanni.

He gave a short head shake. Damned if he knew. "Detective Martin," he said by way of greeting.

"Sir." She nodded, her dark eyes unreadable as ever, then turned her attention to the uniformed officer. "Tenley wasn't the doer. I talked to the warden myself. Damon Tenley is present and accounted for in his cell."

Burton wasn't surprised. But he couldn't deny he'd harbored the smallest, ridiculous hope that Tenley—who was serving life in prison without the possibility of parole for the murder of Raina Noor—had somehow managed to escape from a maximum security facility and kill the woman's husband. That turn of events would make closing the first homicide of the new year a slam dunk.

But it looked like he'd have to let that fantasy die. There was no way Tenley would break out, kill Giles Noor, and then break back *in*. No, someone else had borrowed Tenley's playbook to bludgeon the man. It was the only possibility he could fathom. Any other explanation ... was just too much to accept.

Meredith Vitanni raised her pen. "Sir, the Noor murder was before my time. Did the person who hired Tenley get a life sentence, too?"

It was a solid question. And he could see where Vitanni was headed.

"We never found the contracting party."

Vitanni blinked. "How's that possible. Weren't there bank records or emails or something?"

Martin left her post by the door and ambled over to join them near the bed. "Nope, and nope. The arresting officers found a shoe box stuffed with twenty grand in cash under a loose floorboard in the hall closet outside Tenley's bathroom. *Payment for Noor job* was literally written on the lid. And one of the Noors' hand towels was shoved into the opening with the box. Tenley had taken it from the bathroom."

"Tenley wasn't exactly a genius," Burton added unnecessarily.

"But he never flipped?"

He shook his head. "Never breathed a word. That's why he went away on state charges. Prosecutors said there was no way to meet the federal burden without the other party, or something like that."

"So it's possible the same person who hired Tenley to take out Raina Noor contracted with someone new to kill the husband?" Vitanni mused.

"Six years later?" Martin wanted to know.

Burton raised one shoulder in a shrug. "Why not? If he was a patient man. Or woman."

"It's freaking eerie the way this guy, whoever he is, staged the scene just like the first murder." Martin jerked her chin toward the bronze paperweight being bagged by a white-suited crime scene investigator. "That looks like the same damn paperweight."

The CSI, an affable guy saddled with the name Fredrich Froelich, coughed delicately.

"What's up, FF?"

"The paperweights were a set. The second wife says she could never convince the vic to get rid of them after the first wife's murder. The professor kept the original murder weapon tucked away in a box after the prosecution returned it. This one here was on his desk in the study down the hall because she didn't like looking at it."

Burton eyeballed the female officers. "Is that romantic? Or sick?"

"What, hanging on to the weapon some creep used to do in your wife?" Martin countered.

"Yeah."

She considered it. "Pathetic, mostly."

"Whatever keeping it says about him, let's hope the thing is as fruitful as the first one was," Froelich weighed in.

A bronze paperweight had been found near Raina Noor's body, covered with her blood, some bits of her brain matter, and Damon Tenley's DNA.

"Amen to that, brother."

Martin had a question of her own. "Back up. There's a second wife?"

"Giles Noor remarried eighteen months after the death of his first wife." Vitanni flipped open her notebook. "Hope Noor, the victim's wife, called nine-one-one at approximately twenty-three hundred hours yesterday evening, the eighth of January. She attended her Tuesday evening yoga class with a friend. They stopped for a glass of wine and an appetizer afterward. She dropped the friend off at home a little after twenty two hundred hours and proceeded to her residence."

"This friend corroborates the timeline?"

She nodded. "Yeah, the wife's story checks out. She came home, puttered around in the kitchen, posted some pictures on her social media accounts then went up to bed. Professor Noor was scheduled to teach an early class this morning, so she entered the bedroom quietly and didn't turn on any lights. After attending to her nightly bathroom routine, she slipped into bed next to her husband, who she assumed was asleep. She felt something sticky and turned on the bedside lamp."

The room went silent as the hardened police officers and crime scene technicians imagined the widow's gruesome discovery.

"Damn," someone said low, under his breath.

Burton thought it must've been Froelich. If memory served, he was a newlywed.

Vitanni went on, her mouth set in a thin line. "Hope Noor said nothing appeared to be missing. She's sure the front door was locked when she got home. She gave us a list of people with keys—cleaning service, neighbor who brings in the mail when the Noors are out of town, that sort of thing."

"Where's the wife now?"

"She gave her statement last night. She was pretty wrecked. The social worker on duty had a doctor call in a prescription for a sedative and a uniform took her to the pharmacy to get it then dropped her at the next-door neighbor's place to get some rest. According to the neighbor, she's still asleep."

"You want me to go wake her up?" Martin asked.

Burton frowned. "Let her sleep. He'll still be dead when she gets up." He craned his neck to peer over Froehlich's shoulder. "Are you getting much?"

"It's early. But unofficially? Yeah. It's a physical evidence buffet in here. I already called over to the medical examiner's office to let them know this is coming and it's a high priority."

"Good. Maybe we'll get lucky with the DNA the way you did with Tenley," Vitanni offered.

These young ones all thought DNA evidence was the holy grail, better than an eyewitness, a confession, and fingerprints wrapped up in one. The result of watching too much *CSI* on television, as far as Burton was concerned. DNA evidence was only useful when it matched a known sample. Or when the department had the fairytale budget to go around swabbing large populations of possible suspects, which was exactly never in his experience.

Take Damon Tenley. He hadn't been in the system, but he'd served in the Army, and Uncle Sam had kept a sample. It was pure luck that they got a hit when they ran his DNA.

Burton Gilbert thought he should be so lucky a second time.

CHAPTER THREE

March 2013
Allegheny County Medical Examiner's Office
Pittsburgh, Pennsylvania

Bodhi King removed his helmet, locked his bicycle to the rack outside the employee entrance, and slung his messenger bag across his chest. He breathed deeply to fill his lungs with the urban perfume of exhaust fumes, frying foods, and ground coffee and spices that would be labeled "The Strip District" if the sidewalk vendors lining the slush-covered streets could only figure out a way to bottle and sell it. The lively aromas were a marked contrast to the stagnant formaldehyde-tinged air that would course through his respiratory system for the next nine to ten hours.

He tucked his helmet under one arm and flashed his ID card at the card reader. The hallway was dark and quiet at this hour. He paused outside Saul David's open door. Like Bodhi, Saul was an early riser. They were typically the first two pathologists to arrive each day.

"Morning, Saul." He gave the doorframe a gentle rap with his knuckles.

Saul looked up from the file he was reviewing and swiveled his desk chair to face the hall. "Hiya, Bodhi. Hey, I've got one for you. What did the Buddhist say to the hot dog vendor?"

Even though he knew the punch line, he said, "I don't know, Saul. What did he say?"

"Make me one with everything." Saul beamed at him, waiting for a response.

Bodhi chuckled "Good one."

Their office worker ritual completed, he continued down the corridor to his own office where his boss was lying in wait.

Uh-oh.

Bodhi tried and failed to recall the last time Allegheny County Coroner Jefferson Anderson Jackson

("Sonny" to his friends and enemies alike) had beaten him into work.

"Do you need something, boss?"

"I surely do," Sonny drawled. He eyed Bodhi's bike helmet and his gaze drifted upward. "I trust you've got a brush squirreled away somewhere in your office?"

Bodhi didn't bother to tell him his wild curls weren't tamable. Instead he cocked his head and asked, "Why? Is it yearbook photo day?"

That earned him a gruff laugh. Then Sonny's expression grew somber. "I need you to pinch hit in court today."

"Pinch hit?"

"Thurmont's out with the flu that's been going around, but she's supposed to be testifying at the Tenley murder trial this afternoon."

Victoria Thurmont was a DNA analyst, and a damned good one. He was not.

"I'm not a forensic biologist, sir."

"And I'm not a blooming hydrangea, King. You performed the autopsy on the victim, right?"

"I did. Raina Noor." He never forgot their names.

"You signed the death certificate?"

"Yes."

Sonny gave him a big smile and lifted both hands, palms to the ceiling. "So, no problem, right?"

"It's no problem for me to testify as to my cause of death determination, Sonny. But I'm not qualified to opine on the DNA results."

"Now, son, you know the prosecutor's not gonna ask you anything you can't handle. She said you're already on the witness list."

"I'm on standby for later this week. She seems to think this'll be a quick trial."

Sonny clasped his back. "If you ask me, too quick. Who ever heard of a murder trial going to court in less than six months? Well, it'll be even quicker now. She can put in your testimony as to the cause of death today while she's got you on the stand." He started toward the elevator. "Don't forget to brush your hair."

Bodhi absently ran his hand through his unruly mop, as he watched Sonny walk away. An uneasy tightness clenched his stomach.

The present day

"Earth to Bodhi. I asked if you remember the Tenley case?"

He blinked to bring himself back to the present and his own warm living room. The scent of his blood orange candle overtook the formaldehyde that he could have sworn had filled his nose.

He inhaled, shaking off the memory of Sonny's odd demand. Then he met Saul's eyes. "Yeah, I remember Raina Noor."

"Don't suppose you've caught the news lately?"

"Can't say I have." He smiled but there was no apology in it.

His lack of media consumption was, as the software engineers say, a feature, not a bug. He didn't own a television. He had virtually no online presence—no social media profiles, no online news subscriptions, and an email account he checked sporadically at best.

Saul mumbled something that sounded an awful lot like 'luddite.' "Do you remember her husband?"

"Giles. He was an associate professor at Pitt. In the history department, I think."

"Your memory truly is elephantine."

"Doesn't that just mean large? I'm not sure that's the compliment you think it is."

"Take it as one. Anyway, last week, while you were canoodling with that police chief out in Iowa—"

"Illinois."

Saul shrugged. "Same difference."

"Really, not."

He was about to launch into a description of Onatah, Illinois' distinctive charms, while skirting the issue of Chief Bette Clark's own considerable charms, but Saul's expression stopped him.

"Professor Noor was murdered."

Bodhi was silent for a long moment while he processed the information. Another memory took hold as the image of Giles Noor developed in his mind's eye— grainy at first, then with more clarity.

A t the trial, the prosecutor had called Noor to testify immediately after Bodhi. Out of respect, Bodhi had stayed in the courtroom to listen. Paying witness to Raina and Giles Noor's life together.

Giles was a tall, angular man, stooped with grief. His rounded shoulders made him seem old and frail even though he was only in his early thirties. His faded blue eyes were red and watery throughout his testimony, and his voice quavered. He'd clutched a snowy white hand-

kerchief between his hands while he spoke, twisting it and wringing it repeatedly. But he never broke down and cried. Not until later.

After Noor testified, the judge called for a recess. Bodhi stopped in the men's room on his way back to the office and ran into the overwrought widower. His handkerchief, wet through, rested on the metal shelf above the sink.

Bodhi met his tortured eyes in the mirror and held his gaze.

"It's hard to be the one who's left behind. May your memories be a blessing."

"Thank you, Doctor King," he stammered.

He nodded a goodbye. As a Buddhist, he found condolences difficult to convey with the right speech. But Saul had taught him the traditional Jewish words, and he found them helpful. Although death comes for us all, that didn't take away the grief it left in its wake. It felt right to wish the mourning husband ease and joy in recalling his wife.

Noor called after him. "That bastard going away for life will be a blessing."

Bodhi didn't respond. But Noor got his wish. Raina Noor's murderer ultimately pleaded guilty and was sentenced to life in prison without the possibility of parole.

. . .

He blinked away the memory and looked across the room at Saul. "I'm sorry to hear that."

"Yeah. Well, you haven't heard the half of it," Saul replied.

"Meaning?"

"Meaning, the reason I need your help is this case is a doozy."

He waited for Saul to go on. At this point, all his cases were doozies. He'd retired as a pathologist and now consulted when a responding coroner or medical examiner believed he or she was out of his or her depth. He wasn't called on when the cause of death was clear. Or remotely discernable.

Saul placed his teacup on the low coffee table and leaned forward. "The investigators recovered DNA at the scene, and there was a match in the system."

"That sounds like the opposite of a doozy, Saul. More like a slam dunk."

"It's a match for Damon Tenley."

Bodhi abandoned his teacup, too. "Tenley's out?"

"Nope. He's serving a life sentence in Fayette."

"So ... how?"

"That's what I need you to tell me, hotshot."

Bodhi shook his head. "Come on, Saul. I'm a pathologist, same as you. I can tell you the cause of death, the approximate time, and maybe the weapon. But this biology stuff is way out of my wheelhouse. You know that."

"Sure. But I know how and when the professor was killed. And the weapon the killer used." Saul fell silent, waiting.

After a long moment, Bodhi took the bait. "How?"

"Blunt force trauma. Bludgeoned to death in his bed. With a bronze paperweight."

"Same as Raina."

"Same as Raina."

They stared at each other. Bodhi shrugged.

"What do you want me to say? That it's creepy? Sure. But you need expertise I don't have."

"No. I need you."

"Even if I had the ability to figure out your DNA problem—which I don't—my involvement would be a bad idea. I worked the original case. If the evidence was contaminated then ... no, Saul, it would be a conflict."

"You know the lab's contamination rate is legendary for being so low. Those folks are careful. They always have been, even when Sonny was running the show. For all his faults, and they were legion, he ran a pristine operation."

Bodhi lowered his chin and pinned Saul with a long look. "Oh?"

"Aside from the whole Wally thing, I mean."

"The Wally *thing* never would've happened if Sonny ran a tight ship. A pathologist who destroys autopsy records to further his mistress's political ambitions? That's a loose, leaky ship type of event."

Saul tossed his hands in the air. "Ancient history. I mean, I know he tried to kill your friend, but ... water under the bridge, right?"

"Sorry. Can't help you."

"Aren't you even curious?"

"Not really. The way I see it, someone screwed up six years ago. *Or* more likely someone screwed up the results from the Giles Noor scene. They mixed up the samples with the old ones or something. And that, my friend, is *your* ship, not Sonny's. I don't want any part of destroying your reputation."

Saul's nostrils flared. "My reputation's not at risk. I stand by my office's results. Then and now. There was no contamination, no incompetence, Bodhi. Damon Tenley killed Raina Noor. And *somehow* he's responsible for the murder of her husband. It's crazy, I know. But DNA evidence doesn't lie."

Bodhi sighed. "I can't help you."

"Bodhi—"

Saul's frustration was evident in his voice. Bodhi couldn't resist trying to cheer him up with one of the man's own stupid jokes. "What did the Buddhist coroner put on the death certificate as the cause of death?"

"Life. Ha, ha. I need you to figure out how Tenley's DNA ended up at Noor's murder."

Bodhi watched a fat spider meander up the cracked plaster wall near the window.

Saul gritted his teeth. "Did you hear me? You're the best at solving unsolvable puzzles. And you're an outsider. Squeaky clean, not politically beholden to anyone."

Bodhi stared at the spider as it tried and failed to crawl through the closed window. He crossed the room, pushed up the window, and popped the screen out. The arachnid paused, the pedipalps in front of its legs wriggling at the sensation of the cold air, and then crept toward freedom. He watched it mince through the open window then replaced the screen and shut the window.

Only then did he turn back to his old friend. "I honestly can't."

"There's something you're not telling me."

"Remember Tory Thurmont, the serologist?"

"Sure. She's actually still in the office. She's our senior court-qualified DNA analyst."

"Yeah, well, she had the flu the day she was

supposed to testify at Tenley's trial. And Sonny made *me* fill in."

Saul blanched. Then, like a dog shaking itself dry, he rejected the implication as if it were nothing more than water. "Okay, that's less than ideal, I'll grant you. But there's no question Tenley killed Raina Noor. He confessed."

"Sure, but ... bringing me in on this case is an invitation to reopen the original case, and you know it. The defense bar will be crawling all over you."

"Forget about Raina Noor for a minute. Focus on the new murder. The evidence shows Tenley murdered Giles. I don't know how. But he pulled off the impossible crime. And I'll be damned if I'm going to let him get away with it."

Did Saul have any idea how unhinged he sounded?

"I don't know how I could help. You know what I do. The dead tell me their stories. This is ... different from that."

"This is different from *everything*. That's why I need *you*. You won't approach it as some kind of paint-by-numbers exercise. You'll do ... things. Things that wouldn't occur to the rest of us." He flapped his hands in frustration.

Bodhi focused on his breath. Saul waited. The silence stretched between them. Bodhi wished he were the spider, crawling down the facade of the building, free of the stickier webs formed by human interaction, connection, and history. But he wasn't. He was the fly, and there was no point in pretending otherwise.

"I'm not a wizard, Saul. I'm a pathologist."

Saul screwed up his face. "You're kind of a wizard, too."

To his surprise, a small laugh escaped from his throat. He sighed. "Okay."

"I knew you'd do it."

"Don't start celebrating just yet. You know if I investigate this, I'm going to follow the facts wherever they lead—"

"Sure, sure. Of course."

"Even if they lead me to conclude that someone in your office screwed up. Even if they lead me to conclude that *I* screwed up years ago. Or that *you* screwed up."

"I understand, Bodhi."

"Do you? Really think about it, Saul."

Saul locked eyes with him and nodded. "I wouldn't ask you to look into this if I thought you'd pull your punches. I'm not stupid. I know the press and the public defender's office are gonna have a field day with this. I want an independent investigation that will leave no doubt about the integrity of the medical examiner's office and its results. That's *why* I came to you. I know you'll put the truth before anything, even our friendship."

"As long as you're sure."

"I'm sure. Listen, there's an all hands meeting tomorrow. I'll messenger over the files this afternoon so you can at least skim them beforehand, but don't worry about getting fully up to speed."

"Understood."

He also understood the part Saul wasn't saying—his role at this meeting would be to listen, not speak. Consulting for the medical examiner's office was one thing; sharing his thoughts with the police department and the prosecutor's office wasn't in the cards.

"It'll be just like old times, us working together." Saul stood. "I better get going. I'll send over a consulting contract with the files."

He rose and stretched out his hand. Saul shook it, then pulled him in for a hug. Bodhi patted his shoulder and walked him to the door.

Just like old times.

He waved goodbye from the porch and tried to ignore the knot forming in his gut, an echo of the unease he'd felt six years ago before Tenley's trial.

CHAPTER FOUR

One day later

As Bodhi followed Saul into the vast conference room, he surveyed the people gathered around the elongated oval table. Some faces he knew from his days working for the Allegheny County Medical Examiner's Office. Some were new.

Saul crossed the room and shook hands with a tall redhead wearing a well-tailored dove gray suit and a string of chunky pearls. They exchanged pleasantries, and he gestured for Bodhi to join them by the window.

"Meghan, this is Dr. Bodhi King, formerly of my office. He's the forensics consultant I told you about."

The woman smiled and extended her hand. Her grip was firm, and her warm skin was smooth and soft. "A pleasure." It sounded almost as if she meant it.

"Bodhi, Meghan Ford is the Allegheny County District Attorney," Saul continued with the introductions.

"It's good to meet you, Ms. Ford," Bodhi said.

"Please, call me Meghan. Based on everything Saul's told me, we're lucky to have your services on this one."

"I hope I can prove helpful. From what Saul's told *me*, you folks have an unusual situation on your hands."

She laughed throatily. "That's putting it mildly." She waved a hand over the coffee, tea, and pastry set up. "Help yourself to something to drink and nibble on. We're just waiting on the homicide detectives."

Bodhi bypassed the danishes and fixed himself a cup of green tea. He took the nearest open seat at the table. Saul passed his hands on the back of the chair to his left and continued chatting with the district attorney about some benefit dinner. Bodhi turned to his right and smiled at the dark, slight woman picking apart a roll.

"Long time, no see, Tory."

Victoria Thurmont jerked her head up and blinked at him from behind her cat's eye glasses.

"Bodhi?"

The shock in the forensic biologist's voice surprised him. He assumed Saul would've told his own people that he'd brought their former colleague in as a consultant. Evidently, he hadn't. He wondered why.

"The one and only," he cracked.

"What ... I didn't realize ..."

"I'm consulting," he said to save her from stumbling over the words.

"Oh. I see. It's nice to see you." She mustered a thin smile before returning to her task of ripping chunks of bread from the roll and sprinkling them over the napkin she'd laid out on the table in front of her with no apparent plan to eat any of it.

*She was nervous. But why? She **had** performed the DNA analysis for the Tenley prosecution.*

It would be logical to worry. Even if she stood behind her conclusions, she had to know every step she'd taken in the case was about to be picked apart and pored over ... much like the bread she was in the process of methodically dismantling.

A woman wearing a dark pantsuit and a tall, sturdy African-American man rushed through the door. The man had thick, close-cropped hair shot through with gray. He wore a pair of reading glasses low on his nose and a tie that was askew, its knot loosened.

"Sorry we're late, folks," the man rumbled in a voice Bodhi recognized immediately.

Detective Gilbert from the Homicide Squad seemed to have aged more than the rest of the players in the room. Occupational hazard, maybe?

Bodhi eyed the other detective but couldn't place her.

"Detectives," Meghan bobbed her head in greeting. She moved to stand behind the seat next to Saul's and waited for their attention.

The murmured conversations died, and everyone turned to her as the tardy detectives claimed the closest chairs—near the door, but far from the food and drinks. The female detective's eyes flitted longingly to the coffee. Bodhi watched her calculating whether it was worth the distraction she'd cause if she passed in front of the district attorney to get herself a cup. She caught him watching her and gave him a wry, one-shouldered shrug.

He smiled. He wasn't much of a coffee drinker, but he knew a few. Being in a room with coffee just out of reach would be akin to the torture of Tantalus for more than one of his friends.

Oblivious to the detective's yearning for caffeine, Meghan addressed the room. "We're all here, so let's get started. I trust you all know me. I'd like the rest of you to introduce yourselves, share the organizations you represent, and briefly explain your role in this matter." She smiled coolly, took her seat, and sipped her coffee.

A cheerful Asian man to her left stood. "I'll start. I'm Roland Lee. I'm an ADA working under Meghan. I second-chaired the Tenley prosecution, and I'll be handling any prosecution that might result from the investigation into Giles Noor's murder."

"Second chair? Where's Annette Morris?" Saul asked.

Morris had been the lead attorney during the Tenley prosecution. She was the one who'd prepped Bodhi for trial and had questioned him on the stand. Bodhi had only the faintest recollection of Lee as a silent presence by her side, furiously scribbling notes and handing her exhibits.

"Annette's moved on to more lucrative pastures. She's the general counsel for a pet food company in Tennessee," Meghan explained.

Lee bobbed his head. "But, no worries. I was involved every step of the way. And I pulled Annette's notes out of storage."

Detective Gilbert stood. "I'm Burton Gilbert with the PBP Homicide Squad. I was the lead investigator on the Raina Noor murder, and I'm spearheading the investigation into Giles Noor's murder, as well." He nodded toward the woman sitting next to him.

She popped to her feet, and he introduced her. "This is Detective Martin. She worked the original murder, and she'll be working this one, too."

She nodded, tight-lipped, and sat back down.

Bodhi jerked his chin toward her as Saul began to introduce his team and mouthed '*coffee?*' He was positioned near enough to the drink station that he could get her a cup without disrupting the meeting.

Her grin lit up her face and she nodded eagerly. '*Black,*' she mouthed back.

He stood and slipped behind Meghan's chair. By the time Saul was saying his name, he was back, sliding the ceramic mug across the table to a grateful homicide detective. It was a simple gesture, an act of service which he did gladly and easily. He could see from her smile that it had scored him points. That hadn't been his motivation, but it never hurt to have a friendly face on the team.

"Dr. Bodhi King used to be a pathologist with our department. Now, he's a famous consultant," Saul proclaimed.

One of Bodhi's eyebrows crept up. "Famous might be an overstatement."

"It's not," Tory corrected him. "You're famous in our world, at least." She explained for the benefit of the others. "Bodhi's being modest. He solves unsolvable forensic mysteries. The energy death clusters, those senior citizens who died of fright in the Florida Keys."

"Don't forget the zombies up in Canada," Saul reminded her.

Detective Martin's mouth quirked. "Zombies, eh?"

"It's a long story." Bodhi figured he should wrest control of his resume before Saul mentioned the international agricultural espionage thing in Illinois and accidently revealed confidential national security secrets. "I've been fortunate to be able to help unravel some knotty problems. I hope I can do the same here. Especially because I worked on the Raina Noor murder back when I was with the medical examiner's office."

He expected some reaction from the law enforcement contingent, but they appeared to be unperturbed.

Recognition lit in Roland Lee's eyes. "Of course. I thought I knew you from somewhere."

"Speaking for the district attorney's office, we're happy to have your help on this," Meghan said, reiterating her earlier comment.

"The more the merrier," Detective Gilbert deadpanned in a decidedly un-merry voice.

For now, Bodhi thought.

In his experience, the initial gratitude and acceptance eventually gave way to resistance, if not outright resentment. Very few organizations enjoyed an outsider who questioned their work, rejected their conclusions, or otherwise challenged their authority. He hoped his status as a former colleague would lessen the likelihood that he'd ruffle feathers.

"Thanks. I'm glad to be on the team."

Saul nodded and rubbed his hands together. "Okay, then. Unless the DA's office or the homicide squad has another suggestion, I thought we'd start by answering any questions folks might have about the DNA results."

"We only have one question, Dr. David. How the devil did Damon Tenley's blasted DNA turn up on the murder weapon, the vic, and all over the freaking room when he was miles away, locked in a twelve-by-six cell?" Gilbert's full voice rolled over the room like a wave.

"Just the one, huh?" Saul cracked.

The attempt at humor earned him a handful of soft laughs, but the room crackled with interest as the assembled group leaned forward as one, desperate for an answer.

He eyed Bodhi, who gave a short shake of his head then tilted it right—toward Tory. She was the department's senior DNA serologist, after all. Bodhi had no interest in kicking off the first meeting by making an enemy of her.

Saul blinked his understanding.

"With the caveat that we don't have an answer to

that crucial question *yet*, Ms. Thurmont will walk you through the DNA results. Just a high-level summary, please, Tory."

Her smile stopped well south of her eyes. She shuffled her papers into a tidy pile, tapped her pen on the table, and sipped her water before she spoke.

"The inquiry into the DNA results is proceeding on two simultaneous, but separate, tracks spearheaded by two different teams. The first team is going back through the evidence gathered from the Giles Noor crime scene. Obviously, that's still ongoing, but I can tell you this much: I have zero doubt. It's Damon Tenley's DNA."

"How can that be?" Roland demanded.

She pushed her glasses up the bridge of her nose with one finger and gave the lawyer an even look. "I don't know. All I know is it's a match for his DNA."

"Do you agree, Dr. King?" Gilbert wanted to know.

Every pair of eyes in the room turned to look at him. Tory's were narrowed to slits and her mouth was a tight line. He chose his words with care. "I'm not a DNA expert. But I think everyone who reviewed Tory's original typing report in the Raina Noor case and this new preliminary report would agree that the samples are a match. I don't suppose he happens to be an identical twin?"

"Do twins really have identical DNA?" Martin asked.

"They really do. Well, at least as far as we are able to see," Tory told her. "The issue's come up in criminal cases in other jurisdictions. If Tenley has an identical twin, who also happens to be a murderer, yeah, current DNA typing would come back as a match for both twins. Now, there *is* a new test that claims to be able to distinguish between twins by looking, not at repeat sequences, but for single-nucleotide polymorphisms. In English, that means the test searches for small mutations that occurred after the embryo split in utero."

"Maybe Tenley's twin killed Noor to punish the man he blames for his brother's incarceration?" Lee suggested in a hopeful voice.

Gilbert gave his head a mournful shake. "No such luck. Damon Tenley was an only child. And his parents died in a car accident when he was four. He was raised by distant relatives—his mother's second cousin and her husband, both deceased."

"Natural causes?" Bodhi asked automatically.

The question elicited a humorless chuckle from the detective. "Cancer, both of them."

So much for the evil twin theory. Bodhi'd known it was an impossibly long shot. If Tenley had a twin who could conveniently call the DNA results into question, his defense attorney would have brought it up at trial.

Roland Lee opened his mouth, cut his eyes toward Meghan Ford, and clamped it shut.

"Did you have a thought, Roland?" Saul asked, his tone encouraging.

He reddened. "It's a theory, of sorts. But ... it's pretty farfetched."

"More farfetched than Bodhi's twins theory? I welcome out-of-the-box thinking," Saul reassured him before shooting the district attorney a meaningful look.

She nodded. "Speak your mind, Roland. Heavens knows we're in uncharted territory here."

Lee bobbed his head. "Okay. I just wondered whether someone might be setting him up? Tenley, I mean. Whoever hired him to kill Raina Noor is still out there somewhere. Tenley never gave up the name of the person who paid him. Assuming they've been in contact, could that person have deliberately planted Tenley's DNA at the scene?" He kept his eyes pinned on the table.

Tory's pursed lips twitched from side to side. "It's possible. You know, there was so much DNA, it almost seemed like the killer made no effort to wipe down the room, as if they didn't care that they were leaving so much behind for us to work with."

Meghan asked, "It's not unheard of. Gang members have been known to leave items at crime scenes to mask their DNA and implicate rival gang members. Items of clothing, beer bottles the other guy's touched, that sort of thing. They call them DNA kits." She paused to shake her head at the notion. "Was any other DNA found at the scene?"

"Just the victim's, his wife's, the cleaning crew's. Nothing unexpected."

"Are you running the cleaning people?" Meghan asked the detectives.

"Already done. They came back clean. No records. Nobody's skipped town. No big cash deposits into anybody's account," Detective Martin answered.

The room went quiet. Bodhi got the feeling the detectives had already contemplated Roland's theory—or one very like it—and found it plausible.

When Detective Gilbert broke the silence, he confirmed Bodhi's suspicion. "We'll go out to Fayette and lean on Tenley. I can't imagine he's gonna have a change of heart after all this time, but you never know."

"You should pull his visitor log while you're there," Meghan suggested.

"Ya think?" Martin shot back.

Burton Gilbert placed a hand on her forearm. She slumped back in her chair and clamped her lips together.

"Good idea, Meghan. If this mystery partner did frame Tenley, they'd need to get their hands on a lot of his DNA, right?" he said in a smooth tone, demonstrating a degree of diplomacy that Bodhi hadn't expected.

The district attorney flashed a thin smile.

Tory said, "It wouldn't require buckets of spit or anything. Some people are just 'good shedders.' They leave their DNA everywhere. And studies have shown that some DNA profiles are just ... dominant. On an item that's been touched by, say, six people, one good shedder with strong DNA could overwhelm the other samples."

She waited a moment for the implications to sink in.

Meghan furrowed her brow in thought. She turned back to Tory. "You said there are dual tracks?"

"Right. The second team is reviewing the Raina Noor case for any irregularities." She shot a look at Saul.

He weighed in. "Not that we expect to find any. That case was—is—solid."

Detective Martin pointed her pen at Roland Lee. "Question: Tenley decided to enter a guilty plea to take the death penalty off the table, right?"

"That's right. He pleaded to murder for hire in exchange for life in prison."

"And that happened after Ms. Thurmont testified?"

"Yes—well, no." The prosecutor threw Saul a help-less look.

Bodhi cleared his throat. "Tory didn't testify at Damon Tenley's trial. I did."

"You testified? You're a DNA expert, too?" she pressed.

"No, I'm not. But Tory was sick with the flu, and I was scheduled to testify as to the cause of death. So Sonny Jackson and Annette Morris insisted that I also address the DNA results. I basically read Tory's report and parroted the results on the stand."

He surveyed the reactions around the table. Meghan's face tightened as if she hadn't known. Roland locked his eyes on his legal pad. Tory hunched her shoulders. The detectives exchanged a look he couldn't read. Only Saul seemed unconcerned.

"It was Annette's call," Ronald mumbled.

"That's ... unfortunate," Meghan said in a flat voice.

"Only because we're in this crazy situation," Saul said. "With hindsight, sure, we all wish Annette had pushed back the testimony until Tory was feeling better. But let's not pretend that things like this don't happen. The criminal docket's been swamped since I started at the M.E.'s office. We all know what would have happened if the state had asked for a delay. Defense counsel would've cried to the judge about Tenley's constitutional right to a speedy trial. Having Bodhi step in was a reasonable idea. At the time."

"Sure, at the time. But now, it just adds to the stink on this case," Gilbert groused.

"In what way?" Roland pressed him.

But it was Tory who answered. "Oh, come on, we're all thinking the same thing here. Tenley had no choice but to take a plea after Dr. King testified that the DNA at the crime scene was a match. But now, his alleged DNA turns up at a new crime scene and it turns out the prosecution put up a supposed DNA expert who wasn't even an analyst? Sorry, Bodhi, no offense intended. But it doesn't take a genius to see—"

"—that any attorney with half a brain will say the original DNA evidence is unreliable. Tenley couldn't have killed Giles Noor, and he didn't kill Raina Noor. All he needs to do is file a motion claiming he took the deal even though he was innocent because he was looking at the death penalty if he didn't. He'll recant, ask for a new trial, whatever," Martin finished the grim thought.

"Exactly," Tory agreed.

"It's a possibility," Meghan allowed. "Refresh my recollection—who represented Tenley at trial, Roland?"

"Penelope Geoffries with the public defender's office."

Meghan groaned. "Great. Passionate Penny. She's a true crusader if there ever was one. As soon as she hears about this, she'll find her client an appellate lawyer."

Tory blanched. "Does Tenley's lawyer need to be notified? I mean, the fact that his DNA ties him to a second murder isn't exactly exculpatory, is it?"

Bodhi watched the prosecutors' reactions. Their faces were deliberately blank.

Finally, Meghan said, "That's a decision my office will make in the coming days. You should all hope it doesn't come to that. Any appeal will probably focus on the way the police trample through the crime scenes, contaminating them and making the forensic findings unreliable."

Martin opened her mouth to shoot back but closed it just as fast.

"I'd say this meeting's about done," Saul said in a casual tone as he rose to his feet. "The prosecutors have blamed the police for this situation, the police have blamed my office, and Tory here has suggested it was the prosecutor's screw up. Why don't we stop trying to fix the blame and get out there and fix the problem."

Bodhi tried to hide his grin as he followed his old friend out of the conference room.

CHAPTER FIVE

B urton balanced his cell phone on his thigh and peeked under the table to check the time surreptitiously. Martin had gone down to get a car from the auto pool twenty minutes ago; she'd probably crossed paths with his unexpected visitor in the lobby.

The sedan was probably idling in the lot now, no doubt belching exhaust fumes into the air while the driver drummed her fingers on the steering wheel and cursed Burton for keeping her waiting. Neither image bothered him overmuch: one idling vehicle wasn't going to tip the scales on the environment no matter what the tree huggers said. And the impatient junior detective could damn well cool her heels.

It was critically important not to rush the trembling, teary-eyed woman sitting across from him. But at the same time, it would be an enormous pain in his backside to have to reschedule the interview with Tenley out at the prison. He forced the thought from his mind and focused his attention on Giles Noor's widow.

"Are you sure I can't get you a glass of water or a soda? Our coffee's a few hours old, but I could have someone brew us a fresh pot." He willed her to pass on the coffee. That'd set him back precious minutes.

She shook her head, sending her blonde hair flying, and sniffed. "No, thank you though." She looked up and managed a wobbly smile.

"And you're sure you don't want to talk to a victim's advocate? The social workers are trained to help family members at a time like this." He left unsaid the fact that he was not. He was trained to find the scumbag that put her in this hellish position in the first place.

"You're so kind. I'm ... seeing someone. A therapist, I mean."

"That's good. You're going through a horror most people can only imagine."

The tears she'd been holding back leaked out. "I keep thinking the person who knows what this is like, the person who could really help me, is Giles. But, of course, he's the one who's ... gone."

She ended on a wail and covered her face with her hands.

He waited until she cried herself out. There was nothing else he could do. He couldn't stop the pain welling in her chest. Once her shoulders stopped shaking and the sobs trailed off into a soft hiccupping sound, he scooted his chair closer to hers and put a hand on her arm.

"Mrs. Noor, what is it that I can do for you?"

She wiped her face with the back of her hand and met his eyes. "It's been a week. I just need to know how close you are to catching the monster who did this to ... us."

Nowhere near close.

"The investigation's in full swing, and we're running down every lead. If you're concerned for your safety, I can have a unit assigned to sit outside your house."

Not something he usually suggested for the families, but this case was nothing if not unusual. All he needed was for the ghost who killed her husband to come back and score another victim.

But she sat bolt upright and squared her shoulders. "No. Absolutely not. I mean, thank you, of course. But that's not necessary." The brown eyes widened. "Is it?"

He weighed his response. "I don't think so. Not based on what we know to this point."

Emotion flashed across her face—Fear? Hope? He couldn't tell.

"And what do you know?"

"I can't tell you the specifics, Mrs. Noor. Please understand. I know this is frustrating for you but we have—"

"Do you have a suspect?" Her voice caught.

"Mrs. Noor, I—"

"Please. I need to know. Shouldn't the forensic tests be back by now?" She leaned toward him.

Blast it. She would ask about the forensics. If rookie officers were enamored with the science, civilians regarded it as something approaching magic.

"We do have some preliminary results. But the medical examiner's office is double checking them."

She processed this information with a head tilt and a quizzical look.

"Is that standard?"

He didn't want to tell her. He knew he shouldn't. Not yet. But the woman's husband had been slaughtered in their bed. And their only suspect was behind bars and couldn't have done it.

He blew out a long breath. "No. It's not. But in this case, the forensics team thinks it's prudent."

"Why?"

"How much do you know about ... the first Mrs. Noor's death?"

He watched as her expressive face turned blank and closed. After a moment, she swallowed and spoke stiffly. "Raina was murdered the same way Giles was. He told me how he found her ... laying in the bed, her skull bashed in, blood everywhere. Just ... just like I found him."

Her pale skin went so white she looked translucent for a moment. He gripped her shoulder, afraid she was going to pass out on him.

"Mrs. Noor?"

"S-sorry. I don't understand what you're getting at."

He delivered the news in a flat, matter-of-fact tone. "In addition to the DNA we expected to find—yours and your husband's—preliminary DNA results suggest the presence of Damon Tenley's genetic matter at your husband's death."

She wrinkled her forehead and shook her head. "Damon Tenley? The man who killed Raina? But ... but isn't he in jail?"

"State prison, yes. And he is there. He didn't break out."

"So, his DNA's been there all these years?"

"We're not sure."

Another puzzled look. "But it must've been. You just said ..."

"The DNA experts are reviewing the results to try to figure out what's going on. But this is one heck of a quandary, as I'm sure you can understand."

"Of course. I ... it doesn't make any sense."

That was the understatement of the decade.

"I know. Rest assured, we have a crackerjack team working on it. Please don't share what I've told you with the media or any friends or family. It could compromise our investigation."

She shook her head absently. "I won't. I'm not talking to the press. And I ... I'm alone now. I don't have any family."

He waited a beat. "It's very important that you don't slip and tell a friend, Mrs. Noor."

She turned her brown eyes on him. "I'm not going to say anything. But, surely, you can't think ...." She trailed off, unwilling or unable to complete the thought.

"I'm not sure what to think. That's why I'm heading out to Fayette to talk to the dirtbag myself."

"You're going to the prison?"

"Yes. And, I hate to rush you out, Mrs. Noor. But I made arrangements to interview Tenley this afternoon, and if I miss the appointment we'll have to start from scratch. Bureaucracy, you know."

She scrambled to her feet and tensed as if she planned to bolt from the room. "Oh, of course. Yes, of course. Thank for your time."

"You don't need to thank me. I'm available any time you need to talk. And if you think of anything, anything at all, call me."

"I will." Her eyes darted around the room and she positioned her purse over her shoulder.

He stood. "If you wait a second, I'll walk you out."

"No, no. I've taken enough of your time."

His cell phone vibrated and buzzed in his pocket, insistent and loud. He pulled it out and silenced it. When he looked up, the widow was gone, the door swinging behind her.

He frowned down at the text message from Martin:

Any day now.

He pocketed the phone and turned out the light, hoping he'd been right to share what he knew with Hope Noor.

CHAPTER SIX

Hope stayed in the third floor ladies' room, resting her forehead against the cool tile wall, until a female uniformed officer came in and asked if she was okay.

She nodded weakly and stumbled out the door and into the hallway.

She was very much *not* okay. But she needed to get out of this bland, institutional building. She needed to get home, to a fire in the fireplace, a glass of something that burned on its way down her throat, and a sedative.

She made her way to her car and sat behind the wheel in the visitors' lot, shaking, as wave after wave of nausea built in her stomach, threatened to spill out, and finally subsided. She rifled through her purse for a mint, a stick of gum, anything to take away the sour taste of fear in her mouth.

She didn't know what she'd expected to learn from the gruff homicide detective. But it surely hadn't been that they were looking at Raina Noor's killer as a suspect. It defied all logic and common sense. Not to mention physics.

She managed a long, shaky breath.

Pull it together, Hope. They'll rerun the tests and say it was a mistake. The DNA they found was old, leftover from the first murder. Right?

Right, she assured herself, staring at her red, swollen eyes in the compact she'd pulled from her purse during her fruitless search.

All she had to do was stay calm. Her heartbeat slowed and her pulse settled to a normal rate. She turned the key in the ignition and eased the car out of the parking space at a crawl. She didn't quite trust herself to drive. But, as she was reminded for the umpteenth time since Giles' death, she was alone in this world now.

You're doing this to yourself, she chided, as she crept into the flow of midday traffic. It was true. Becca from yoga or Oliver from the garden club or any one of her former coworkers or current neighbors would be happy to help her out.

Hadn't they all swooped in, their arms full of

casseroles, flowers, and fruit baskets, to share their tear-ful, sweet stories about Giles? And still, every day, a new cascade of sympathy cards poured through the mail slot in the door and fanned out across the entryway. So many of the mourners mentioned Raina's death, hesitantly, but determinedly. It was as if they didn't want to offend her but couldn't let the pair of violent deaths go unmentioned.

She understood the impulse. She'd been thinking about Raina an awful lot since Giles' death, herself. The residue of the grief Giles had carried with him in the years since Raina's death overlapped with Hope's own regret and pain. It all mixed together in her foggy brain. At least he'd had her, Hope, to help him through the aftermath.

As she followed the strand of her grim thoughts, the car swerved across the yellow line into on-coming traffic. A blare of a horn blasted her back to the present. She jerked the wheel and yanked the car back into her lane, sweat beading on her forehead, her vision blurred and dim. She lowered the window so the cold air stung her face, clenched her jaw, and straightened her spine.

Next time she needed to go out, she'd ask Mrs. Remmy across the street to give her a lift. She shouldn't be driving anyway, not with the mix of tranquilizers and antidepressants—some prescribed, some scavenged from

Giles' nightstand, remnants of his own nightmare after Raina's murder.

For now, she just needed to make it home alive so she could curl up in bed. If she was lucky, the sleeping pills would bring her a dreamless sleep instead of one haunted by Damon Tenley's dark, hollow eyes and thin, pale face.

CHAPTER SEVEN

"Pigs blow their coats twice a year."

Bodhi stood in the doorway to Tory Thurmont's lab and made the pronouncement.

She raised her head from the rows of data she was reviewing and blinked at him.

"Pardon?"

"Mind if I come in?"

She made a welcoming gesture with her hand. He stepped inside and perched on a tall stool across the table from her.

"That's what it's called when a pig sheds—blowing its coat."

"Okay? And ..."

"And pigs usually blow their coats in the summer, but for some reason Snickers is doing it now, in January."

She rested her pen on her desk and folded her hands in her lap. "I have so many questions."

"I'll bet. Fire away." He smiled.

"You have a pig ... named Snickers?"

"No, I don't have any pets. But when I got back into town last Friday, I started housesitting for a friend who has a macaw."

"Where were you?"

"Pardon?"

"You said were out of town."

"Oh, right. I've been spending a lot of time in Illinois, pretty much splitting my time between here and there. I've been renting my house out since ... I left the office. Anyway, my tenant had to travel for work, so I came back to pet sit and take care of the place for her."

"You're a pretty nice landlord."

He shrugged. "Anyway, over the weekend, I had to take Eliza Doolittle to the vet."

"Eliza Doolittle ..."

"The macaw."

"Of course."

Tory grimaced and pinched the skin between her eyes together with two fingers.

"Do you have a headache?" he asked, forgetting about his story for the moment.

She shook her head and exhaled slowly. "It's just tension. I've been staring at these numbers for hours. A story about Eliza Doolittle the macaw and a pig named Snickers is exactly what I need. It'll be better than acetaminophen."

He frowned. "Still, you should get up and move around." He crossed the room to the stainless steel sink and filled a clear plastic cup with water from the tap. "Rehydrate."

She took the cup two-handed, drained it, and placed it on the table. Then she stood, rolled her neck from side to side, and twisted her shoulders. "Thanks. But you can't leave me hanging."

"Right. So, pretty much from the time I got to the house, Eliza Doolittle started sneezing ... a lot. I made an appointment with her vet and took her in on Saturday morning."

"Oh, no. Is she okay?"

"Yeah. Turns out she's reacting to my incense. I stopped burning it, and she stopped sneezing."

"And Snickers the pig factors into this tale how exactly?"

"We met Snickers and his littermate Snowball in the waiting room. Their owner was checking out when we checked in at the front desk. I rubbed their bellies for a bit. Eliza Doolittle wasn't impressed. She was in her cage up on the counter. She turned her head to the wall and ignored the entire scene."

"A bit of a diva, huh?" Tory grinned.

"You could say that. Anyway, this morning, four days later, while she was preening, she pulled this stiff, wiry fur out of her feathers and spat it on the floor. I'll give you three guesses what it was."

"Pig fur?"

"Pig fur. Now here's the thing. Eliza Doolittle never got close to the pigs. And the avian veterinarian has a dedicated exam room. The pigs hadn't been in that room."

"Was there a technician or assistant who might have treated Snickers and Snowball?" The biologist seemed to have forgotten her headache, caught up in the avian-porcine drama.

"It's possible. But Eliza Doolittle preens her feathers all the time. There's no way she's had pig fur stuck in her plumage for a week and didn't tend to it. She blamed me, by the way."

"Blamed you how?"

"She squawked at me and called me a 'dirty bird.'"

Tory giggled. "Harsh. Maybe you had some fur on your hands and transferred it to her feathers when you took her out or put her back in her cage."

"A plausible explanation," he agreed. "But I cleaned

her cage thoroughly as soon as we got home from the vet's office and she's had a bath since then, too."

"So what's your theory?"

"Secondary transfer."

Tory thought for a moment. "An indirect transfer."

"Right. I must've left pig fur somewhere in the house —it fell off my sweater or something—and she picked it up while she was flying around."

"Sure, okay. As fun as this story is, does it have a point?"

"I need a primer on secondary DNA transfer. I read some journal articles last night, but this isn't my area of expertise."

"You think there was an indirect secondary transfer of Tenley's genetic material to the crime scene?"

"Maybe? I think it's more plausible than this mystery partner murdering Giles and planting Tenley's DNA at the scene. And I *know* it's more plausible than Tenley actually managing to get out and murder the man. So, yes, I think it's worth exploring."

She tapped her pen against her front teeth, apparently lost in thought. After a moment, she nodded, a smart bob of her head, and unearthed a white board and a marker from a drawer.

She wrote *contamination* and *transfer* on the board in small, neat printing then shot him a knowing look.

"I'm going to start with the basics. But don't be modest. If you already know what I'm telling you, let me know, and we'll skip it. Just so you know, I'm not buying your 'aw, shucks, I'm just a humble forensic pathologist' shtick. Your reputation precedes you, Bodhi."

"Noted. Although it's not an act. I'm no geneticist."

"Contamination and transfer are both problems that, funnily enough, result from advances in analysis. They're problems of success. In the old days, before my time, an analyst needed some *thing* to use to detect DNA: a drop of saliva, a speck of blood, some semen. Something tangible. But, since the late nineties, we haven't needed bodily fluid. Trace DNA is left behind on anything a person touches. Especially if they happen to be a good shedder, we can get their DNA from a surface or an item they handled."

"That revolutionized forensics."

She sighed. "It did. But the sensitivity of the testing also opened up the Pandora's Box of contamination and transfer. Take contamination. Contamination happens when a sample is compromised at some point between collection and testing. It's the result of sloppy police or lab work. Someone who handled the sample adds their trace DNA to the sample because they failed to use proper procedure. Transfer is a different problem."

"Quick question. The Phantom of Heilbronn—contamination or transfer?"

She smirked. "You're no geneticist, but you just happen to know about the Phantom of Heilbronn, huh? That debacle was an example of contamination. For years, German police chased a female serial killer. Her DNA was linked to an array of crimes, including six murders, drug deals, robberies, break-ins, you name it. She committed crimes all over the country and in other parts of Europe. The only problem?"

"She didn't exist."

"Right. Well, she does exist. She just wasn't a criminal. She was a factory worker who packaged the cotton swabs used to collect DNA samples and left traces of her own genetic material on the swabs she handled. I know I just said contamination happens during collection and testing. I guess the Phantom of Heilbronn is the exception that proves the rule. That contamination happened at the very beginning of the process, during manufacturing. Which means, I suppose, it could happen even earlier. Maybe some day a cotton picker's DNA will turn up at a crime scene."

"So that's contamination. How's transfer different?"

"Unlike contamination, which is the direct, accidental addition of extraneous DNA, transfer's unavoidable. We all leave pieces of ourselves behind. Studies show that we shed more than fifty million skin cells every day, and each cell leaves behind some trace DNA. Then there's sneezing, kissing, you name it. The world is awash in unseen genetic material."

"This is what you were talking about yesterday at the meeting, right? The studies with the good shedders who touched the same item?"

"That's part of it. That's primary transfer. A husband kisses his wife before she leaves for work. Now his DNA is on her lips. That's the DNA we want to find at crime scenes. The problem is secondary transfer, which happens when a person's DNA is detected on something he or she *hasn't* touched."

"Like Eliza Doolittle having pig fur in her feathers. She didn't touch Snickers."

"Right. But someone or something that did touch the pig transferred the fur to her. In the husband and wife example, let's say the wife has lunch with her old college roommate later in the day and they kiss each other on the cheek. Now the roommate has her friend's husband's DNA on her face. If she, heaven forbid, is attacked and strangled on her way home from lunch, maybe the attacker leaves behind his DNA. But maybe he doesn't. Maybe he wears gloves. The crime scene team swabs her face and neck and gathers a sample. Now, the husband's

DNA from that innocent kiss hours earlier makes him a suspect."

"What about the wife? Her DNA is there, too, isn't it?"

"Maybe, maybe not. Some people are bad shedders. They don't leave much, if any, genetic material in their wake."

He was silent for a moment, considering all the possible permutations. "How long can DNA survive? What if the lunch date happened a day or more after the kiss? Would the husband's DNA still show up?"

"Unlikely. Presumably the wife's brushed her teeth or drank some liquids in the interim. But under the right conditions, on the right surface, DNA could survive for *years*."

"Wait. Then it's still possible that Tenley's DNA has been in Noors' bedroom ever since Raina's murder?"

She lifted her shoulder. "Yes, it's possible. But none of Raina's DNA turned up on the new samples. I tend to think Detective Martin's got it right. If the house was thoroughly cleaned, I wouldn't expect a ticking time bomb of Tenley's DNA to be nestled in place all these years."

He ran through a series of possible explanations in his mind and landed on one that seemed plausible. "So if one of the responding officers had been out to the prison earlier in the day, he or she could've touched something that had Tenley's DNA on it and brought it with them to the Noors' house."

"Sure. Or it could even be a case of tertiary transfer. A police officer who *didn't* respond to the scene might've been at SCI-Fayette and picked up Tenley's DNA. That person could've transferred it to a squad car that a responding officer later drove. Or they could've touched the buttons on the same vending machine as Martin or Gilbert or drank from the same water fountain as Fred Froelich. The possibilities are endless."

"So you think it's a case of transfer?"

She frowned, her mouth a thin line. "I hope that's what it is. It's the explanation least likely to set off a firestorm of in-fighting or to help Tenley weasel out of his sentence. But it's going to take some legwork to prove. And I need to rule out an error first."

He rested a hand on her shoulder. "I can start running down the possible vectors who might've had contact with Tenley's DNA. You focus on the science."

She gave him a halfhearted smile. "Thanks."

He held her gaze for a beat. "Can I ask you something else? I don't want it to sound like an accusation because it isn't. I'm just trying to sort out which facts are relevant."

"Sure." She answered instantly, but her voice was anything but certain.

"Okay. Did you really have the flu the day you were supposed to testify at Tenley's trial?"

She bristled. "Of course I did. Are you suggesting I'm a malingerer?"

"Not at all." He hesitated. "But I remember how Sonny ran the office. He had ... uh ... definite opinions. I wondered if he might have pressured you to overstate your conclusions or something."

"Tenley confessed, remember?" she said hotly.

"He was staring down some pretty damning DNA evidence. Entering a guilty plea to take the death penalty off the table could've been attractive even if he was innocent," he said levelly.

"Take it up with the legislature if you're opposed to capital punishment. But to answer your question, Sonny wasn't pressuring me." She paused and lifted an eyebrow. "Annette Morris was."

***

"Did you know the district attorney leaned on Tory to overstate the DNA results at Tenley's trial?"

Saul's head jerked up and he swiveled his chair away

from his computer monitor to give Bodhi his full attention. "Meghan did what?"

"Not Meghan, Annette Morris. Tory says Annette was adamant that she interpret the DNA profile as establishing that the odds of someone other than Tenley being the killer were 1 in 3 million, more than double the population of the entire county. And ten times the city population. I mean, think about that."

Saul's nostrils flared. He closed eyes for a second before he choked out a strangled response. "Yes, I know the population statistics. But, no, I wasn't aware the DA's office was leaning on Tory."

"That's why she called off the day of the trial. She says she *was* sick to her stomach, but it was more of a case of nerves than influenza."

Saul muttered darkly under his breath.

"Do you want the good news?" Bodhi asked.

"No, Bodhi. I'm only interested in news that'll ruin my day. Bad news or no news, that's my motto."

Bodhi flashed him a half-grin. "Tough. The good news is that Annette didn't have much time to prep me when I stood in for Tory. I literally read the conclusion in Tory's report, word for word. She didn't follow-up with any cute questions, probably because she knew my answer would be 'I don't know.' We spent most of my time on the stand going over my prepared testimony as to the cause of death."

Saul exhaled. "That is, in fact, good news. Did she try to shape your conclusions at all?"

"Not that I recall. No more so than any prosecutor does. I remember the witness prep being unremarkable."

"Was Lee involved in this little plan of Annette's?"

"Tory and I both think not. Annette treated Roland as a glorified legal assistant. He didn't have much of a role at the trial."

"Small mercies."

"Yeah. But it does raise the question of why she was willing to take the risk to get a conviction. I know the DNA evidence was the sexy part, but let's not forget the box of cash. Isn't that the most damning part?"

Saul shook his head. "You wouldn't have known this, but Penny Geoffries filed a motion in limine to keep that box full of money out of evidence and the judge granted. The jury wasn't ever going to hear about that cash payment."

"On what grounds?"

"Bad search. The police had an arrest warrant based on the DNA results, but they never bothered to get a search warrant."

"What a mess."

"It's no messier than any other criminal case, and we

both know it. The only difference is that this is the case where we're turning over the rocks and finding the foul creatures that live underneath."

"Fair enough."

"But it does mean we need to try our darnedest to keep Giles Noor's murder separate from the Raina Noor case. It'll be bad for everyone involved if Tenley gets a new trial."

"Bad for everyone but Tenley, you mean."

Saul tightened his jaw. "Bodhi, so help me, don't even think about going all non-attached Buddhist on me."

"I warned you I plan to follow where the truth leads."

Saul let out a great whoosh of breath. "That's true, you did. And I retained you to explain Giles Noor's death, not to rehash Raina Noor's. Before you say it, yes, I know you can't figure out one without better understanding the other. I get it. But please focus on the present, Bodhi. Please. I swear to you if you happen to turn up evidence that clears Tenley in the first murder, I'm not going to sit on it. I'll go see that public defender myself. But please, just deal with the current headache instead of going off and poking under rocks with a stick."

Saul's suffering was real. It was etched across his

face in stark lines, and it rang in each word he spoke as he pleaded with Bodhi.

"Okay. I hear you, and I get it. You have my word."

"Thank you."

"That said, I need to speak to Damon Tenley."

"What? No. Gilbert and Martin are meeting with him now. They'll brief us. Besides, how does talking to Tenley fit in with what you just agreed to do?"

"Saul, I'm not a mystic. I have the same training as you. The reason I've been able to solve these so-called unsolvable forensic mysteries is that I ask the dead to tell me their stories, then I listen."

"Sounds pretty mystical to me."

Bodhi shrugged. "You want an answer, don't you?"

"Sure. But, Damon Tenley's off limits. So go commune with Giles Noor's corpse. Do you want me to find out where he's buried?"

"Wait, Noor's already been interred? Was he Jewish?"

The Jewish faith required burial as soon as possible after death, and it discouraged autopsies. When Bodhi had worked at the medical examiner's office, policy had been to expedite the autopsies when the deceased was an observant Jew. It had been Saul's idea, but Sonny had grudgingly agreed, and the office had seen an increase in cooperation from the Jewish community.

"Bingo. Mrs. Noor isn't Jewish, but she insisted we follow the procedures for her husband. We had his autopsy completed by noon on Wednesday, and I believe he was buried later in the day—less than twenty-four hours after he died."

Bodhi frowned, remembering. "But I performed Raina Noor's autopsy. I would've remembered it if had been expedited."

"Apparently, Giles wasn't particularly devout. He was what I call a cultural Jew. But, according to the second Mrs. Noor, after they married, he grew increasingly religious." Saul gave a philosophical shrug. "It happens. Especially after a loss like the one he suffered."

"I guess. It's interesting Hope Noor didn't share his faith. I wonder what the story is there?"

"Hmm, I have no idea."

An idea niggled in the back of Bodhi's mind. "You don't have a problem with me talking to Hope Noor, do you?"

A wave of relief broke across Saul's face. "Now you're cooking with gas. Yes, go talk to Hope Noor. Make some headway on *this* case."

"Great. Will do." Bodhi smiled and gave a small wave goodbye.

"Oh, hang on. Mona wanted me to invite you over for dinner one night this week. How about tomorrow?"

"Sure. I'd love to."

"Great. We can leave from here. I'll give you a ride home afterward. Unless you want to bring someone."

"Bring someone?"

"A date, Bodhi. A lady friend. Or are you and your police chief exclusive?"

Bodhi blinked. He hadn't devoted much time to analyzing his relationship with Bette Clark. She was tied to Onatah, Illinois. He was tied to ... nowhere. They hadn't discussed a shared future. They'd spent their time together hiking and stargazing; snowshoeing; and cooking and eating. He had no idea whether he considered them to be exclusive, let alone if Bette did. The topic had never come up.

Saul coughed, pulling him back to the present.

"Sorry. I was lost in thought."

"I noticed," Saul said in a dry voice that hinted at amusement.

"Uh, no plus one."

"Okay, then. It'll be you, me, Mona, and the young Davidlings."

"Great." Bodhi smiled absently and backed out of the office, occupied with thoughts of a tall, lean police chief with silvery locks, clear, sharp eyes, and a laugh like bourbon laced with honey.

CHAPTER EIGHT

B urton shifted his bulk in the molded plastic chair, searching in vain for a moderately comfortable position. He stole a glance at Chrys, who appeared to find the prison visiting room furniture more than adequate. That, he thought sourly, is the difference between being a six-foot-two, two-hundred-pound middle-aged man and a spry young woman.

Just how youthful was she? He wondered. In recent years, he'd noticed the rookies were getting younger and younger. He was pretty sure the department was now recruiting them directly out of middle school. It was the only possible explanation.

She cut her eyes toward him and spoke out of the

side of her mouth. "I still can't believe you told the widow about Tenley."

Oh, good. She wanted to put this downtime to use arguing.

"She asked for an update, Chrys. I felt she deserved one. She's going to keep it to herself."

Chrys laughed softly. "The chivalrous Burton Gilbert rides to the rescue of yet another damsel in distress."

"What's that supposed to mean?" His tone came out gruffer than he'd intended, but screw it.

Her expression clouded with worry. "Nothing. I'm sorry, Burton. I didn't mean anything by it. Why don't we drop it?"

Drop it? Not a chance. If the book on him around the squad was he was some fuddy-duddy dinosaur who treated the ladies with kid gloves and a side of sexism, he darn well needed to know. Especially these days, in this climate.

He was opening his mouth to press her, when a corrections officer banged into the room with Tenley in tow.

"Detectives," the officer said. "The warden said to set you folks up in a private room but we don't have one free. We can keep this room cleared for another twenty or thirty minutes, though."

He propelled Tenley into a free chair across the table from Burton and Chrys. Tenley sat down, leaned back, and stretched out his legs under the table. He grinned lazily.

"That's fine," Chrys told the guard. "As long as we're not keeping a bunch of families waiting."

He shrugged. "Ever since the state started the virtual visiting program, in-person visits have dropped off by a lot. Can't say I blame folks. Who wants to drive out to this hellhole and go through the pat down and search just to sit in one of those miserable chairs and try to make themselves heard over the din of all the other visits when they can have a video visit from the comfort of some satellite office and actually hear what their inmate's saying. Right, Tenley?"

Tenley shrugged. "I wouldn't know. I don't get any visitors—real or virtual."

The guard twisted his mouth in acknowledgment and nodded. Burton blinked. He'd spent enough time in the state's various correctional facilities to recognize the grudging ... respect was the only word for it ... between the officer and the inmate. It came as something as a surprise. Usually, lifers like Tenley mellowed out at some point in their second decade of incarceration, realized this was their new home and made the best of it.

But Tenley'd only been locked up for a little under

six years. Burton had expected him to still be seething, making his bones, and playing the tough guy. Apparently not.

The next words from the correctional officer took away any doubt. "The duty lieutenant said there's no reason to have him cuffed during the interview unless you guys feel it's necessary."

He held the handcuff key in his right hand, waiting for the go ahead to unlock the bracelets around Tenley's' wrists.

Beside him, Burton felt Chrys' surprise.

"We're not worried about this lowlife," he told the guard. "Go ahead and take them off."

Chrys stiffened. He kept his posture relaxed. They'd checked their guns on their way in, so it wasn't as if Tenley could overwhelm them and grab a weapon. And he was pretty sure the interview was unlikely to devolve into a hostage situation with three law enforcement personnel and one inmate. It was better not to show any sign of intimidation or concern.

The guard nodded and Tenley held out his wrists. After the cuffs came off, Tenley made a show of rubbing his skin. Chrys rolled her eyes.

Burton glanced up at the guard. "Are you planning to stick around?"

"Yes, sir. Unless you want me to leave. But given how open the area is, protocol would be to stay."

"Yeah, find yourself a seat somewhere nearby and get comfortable. I don't expect we'll be here long."

Tenley cocked his head. "You drove all the way out here for a quickie?"

It was addressed to both of them, but his eyes lingered on Chrys.

Burton tensed, ready to tear into Tenley, but stopped himself. Protecting the female detective sitting next to him would make her seem weak and play into her comment about his white-knight complex. He gritted his teeth.

Meanwhile, Chrys bared hers. "Let's get something straight, Damon. Detective Gilbert and I didn't come out here to brighten up your dull existence. I don't give a crap if you never get visitors. And I'm not impressed that Officer O'Hagen over there and the warden don't think you needed to be restrained. They're comparing you to a population of lying, thieving, raping, drug-dealing, murderous dirtbags. Me? I compare you to something I'd scrape off the bottom of my shoe. And you're the less appealing of the two."

Tenley lifted his eyebrows, but Burton noticed he also sat up straighter.

He guessed they'd established who'd be playing good cop and who'd be bad cop during this interview.

He gave Tenley an easy smile. "Sorry about my partner. She's got a bit of a temper. You know how the ladies can be."

Tenley narrowed his eyes, unsure how to respond.

"Nah, he didn't kill Raina Noor to shut her up. That was about the money. Right, Damon? All in a day's work." Chrys interjected.

Tenley flushed. He caught his top lip between his front teeth and bit down.

"What's the matter, Damon? Does Detective Martin have it all wrong?"

"Yes," he growled. "She does."

"So, set us straight. It wasn't murder for hire?"

Tenley closed his eyes, and Burton watched the muscles in his face slacken. The inmate inhaled deeply through his nose and exhaled softly through his mouth. As he repeated the breathing sequence, Burton shot Officer O'Hagen a questioning look.

"Mindfulness meditation. They teach it to them as an anger management tool." He shrugged.

"We shoulda sent that Buddhist coroner out here," Chrys whispered out of the side of her mouth.

After another in-breath and out-breath, Tenley opened his eyes and cleared his throat.

"I was paid. I didn't kill her for the money. Or out of any personal animosity."

"Personal animosity—did you eat a dictionary?" Chrys badgered him.

He didn't react.

Burton chimed in, "Okay, if you didn't have a grudge against Raina Noor, and the money was just a nice side benefit, why'd you do it? Did you do it to get at her husband?"

Tenley frowned and shook his head.

"What, then? You're just a violent psychopath who did it for kicks?" Chrys pressed him.

"I did it as a favor for someone." He blurted the words. Then he clamped his jaw shut and stared at them, wide-eyed, as if he was as surprised as they were to hear the words come out.

"A favor for who?" Burton asked.

"Whom," Chrys corrected him. "Don't forget you're talking to a learned professor, detective."

Tenley's expression flattened.

"Hey, is that what it was about, Damon? Were you jealous of Professor Noor? He was a respected academic with a gorgeous wife, nice house in Squirrel Hill, all the things you didn't have?"

"No. I told you it was a favor. And I'm not saying

anything more about it." He crossed his arms over his chest to drive home the point.

Burton waited a beat. "This person you did the favor for—they really hated the Noors though, right? I mean, they must've if they asked you to kill the wife. Here's the real question: did they hate them enough to wait seven years to finish the job?"

Tenley lowered his chin and pitched forward, squinting hard. "Wait. Noor was killed?"

"Murdered, actually. Bludgeoned to death with a bronze paperweight while he lay in bed—is this ringing any bells, yet?" Chrys asked.

Tenley shook his head like a toddler refusing peas. "No, no. You're lying."

"Do you honestly think we have nothing better to do with our time, Damon?"

"But ... who—?"

"Believe me, if we knew that, we wouldn't be sitting in this hellhole with you. Despite what you think, this isn't a social call."

Tenley turned his attention from Chrys and wheeled toward Burton, wild-eyed. "I don't know who killed that guy. I didn't even know he was dead. You gotta believe me."

"See, that's the thing. We think you do know. The way we see it, with you in a cage, the most likely suspect is … well, you're no dummy, you can figure out the rest."

"What? No, I don't know anyone who would—"

"Sure you do. Your partner. The person who paid you twenty grand to do Raina Noor."

Tenley laughed. "No way. You guys are way off base."

Burton eyeballed the inmate.

Tenley's hunched shoulders unfolded and loosened, and his tight, furrowed forehead smoothed out. "Way off base," he repeated gleefully.

"Enjoy it while you can, Damon. We've got a whole new crime scene to process. And forensic testing's only gotten better since we put you away. Sooner or later we're going to find this dirtbag."

Tenley shrugged. "Good luck with that."

Chrys stood up and pushed back her chair. "We don't need luck. It's as good as done with or without you."

"Right."

Burton lumbered to his feet and pressed his palms down on the table. He loomed over Tenley. "You have lots of time in here to think. Spend some of it considering how this could play out for you. You help us out—give us a name—and you'll be helping yourself out."

Tenley scoffed.

"Listen, I'm not promising the DA could do anything about your sentence, but there are other privileges that could be arranged. Maybe a transfer?"

"Here's the thing, detectives. I've made my peace with my life. I know full well I'm going to die in a cage like a rat. But, you know what? I have my books, my classes, my job. I'm paying the price for what I did to Raina Noor. My conscience is as clear as it's gonna get. So, I mean it—good luck finding Professor Noor's killer. But don't come out here again. I have nothing to say to you."

O'Hagen escorted Tenley back to his cell and told Burton and Chrys he'd be right back.

"Just wait a second," he said on his way through the door. "The warden wants a word."

"Good," Chrys said under her breath as a loud buzzer sounded and the pair disappeared behind a thick metal door. "I'd like a word myself."

"Mmm-hmm," Burton agreed absently. "Hey, you remember that coroner who tried to kill Saul and Bodhi?"

"Yeah, Dr. Stewart or something like that."

"He's serving time here, too. Almost got out early for good behavior about a year and a half ago."

"What happened?"

Burton quirked a smile. "It was the darnedest thing.

That little lawyer he stabbed, the McCandless gal, came out here to see him. Wanted to see if he was rehabilitated. He ended up lunging for her, and she head-butted him in the face. Broke his cheekbone. Probably happened right here," he mused, surveying the room.

C hrys was still chuckling when O'Hagen returned.

"Most people don't find this room so entertaining," he remarked.

"Detective Gilbert was just filling me in on an attempted attack that ended with the inmate getting head-butted in the face. I thought it was funny, although I might have a perverse sense of humor," Chrys allowed.

O'Hagen smile appreciatively. "That's the only kind that keeps you sane in a job like this. Yeah, I heard about that little lawyer who broke Wally Stewart's face. He had it coming. He almost pulled one over on the system. Played the model prisoner. But I never bought it. You could tell it was an act. Not like Tenley."

"Excuse me?"

"Damon Tenley is a model prisoner. Oh, he doesn't brown nose the counselors the way Stewart did or try to charm the teachers or anything. He just keeps his head down and his mouth shut, keeps to himself, and does what he's told."

"He's a stone-cold killer," Chrys objected.

"With all respect, detective, nobody in here's a Boy Scout. It's a sliding scale, like."

"He's trying to tell you they grade on a curve, Martin," Burton added.

"Still." She set her mouth in a line Burton recognized all too well.

"Are you going to take us to the warden's office?" Burton asked.

"Actually, he's on his way down. This room's still blocked off on the schedule, and if he comes to you, you don't have to go any deeper into the bowels of this place. You know, you probably don't have a fan club here."

That was an understatement if Burton ever heard one. He estimated that the homicide squad had probably arrested a good forty or more of the residents. And while they were in plainclothes and weren't wearing or carrying anything that identified them as police detectives, inmates always knew. Once, one had hocked a loogie at him down at the old Western Penn prison and yelled that he could smell the cop on him.

"Works for me," Burton said, depositing himself back in the wretched chair.

"Here he comes now," O'Hagen said, peering

through the plate-glass window that filled the opposite wall.

Burton hoisted himself back out of the seat, ignoring his knees' complaints.

Warden Doug Hardiman looked like a college professor, complete with tortoise shell glasses and sweater vest. But Burton had heard his nickname was Hard Ass Man, so he assumed the man's appearance didn't tell the full story.

"Detectives," he said cheerfully, as he crossed the scuffed floor. "Thanks for waiting."

"It's our pleasure, sir," Burton said.

"Detective Chrysanthemum Martin, sir," Chrys said, sticking out her hand. "We spoke on the phone."

"Ah, yes, Detective Martin, nice to see you. And, of course, I know Detective Gilbert. He's been kicking around the system longer than I have," the warden laughed as he pumped Chrys' hand.

"Holding out for that pension," Burton said, extending his own hand.

"You and me both, Burt," Hardiman confided.

"I hear that. Thanks for making Tenley available, Doug. We appreciate it."

"Happy to help the boys"—a glance at Chrys—"and girls in blue. Was Damon helpful?"

"Not really, sir," Chrys answered.

Hardiman frowned. "That surprises me. Mr. Tenley's been something of a ... well, I don't like to use the phrase 'model prisoner,' as I think it gives people the wrong idea ... but that's what he's been. He more or less does the right thing and keeps quiet about it. Not looking for any gold stars."

The warden's assessment of Damon Tenley squared with O'Hagen's. This time, Chrys didn't bother to protest. But Burton was about to ask Hardiman to stretch the rules to just shy of their breaking point, so he did dig into the statement.

"No beefs with other inmates? No contraband? Nothing?"

Hardiman shook his head. "No. He was aggressive when he was first processed in. A couple lunchroom fights, some pushing in the yard. That's fairly standard. The new guy needs to establish right at the outset that he takes no crap. Otherwise, he makes himself a target. I don't condone it, but I understand it. But, after that, once he made it clear that you messed with him at your peril, he settled down fast. Some of the gangs approached him, wanted him to join, but he passed. Without incident, I might add, which is rare. No, Damon Tenley's a loner who tries not to get noticed. You can tell he served in the military. He's disciplined, respects authority."

"Except for that whole murder thing," Chrys said, apparently unable to keep her tongue in line.

"Nobody becomes a long-term guest of the commonwealth because of their good decision-making skills. And, I don't know his service history, but I know he saw action. Some of those guys come back with an itchy trigger finger." Hardiman shrugged. "Mind you, I'm not making excuses. It's just the reality."

Burton saw the opening he needed. "Fair enough. Do any of his old army buddies visit? Call?"

Hardiman stroked his chin while he thought. "Not that I know of. Not offhand."

"Could you have someone look into it? Pull his call records and the visitor logs, and maybe the recordings of his telephone calls, as far back as you keep them?"

Hardiman shrugged. "Sure. I'll just need a copy of the subpoena to send to the state's attorney."

Burton and Chrys exchanged a look, which was not lost on Hardiman.

"Come on, detectives. You know these fellas have rights even in here."

"We could get a subpoena, Doug. I have no doubt a judge would sign it, but it's complicated. It dredges up ancient history." Burton used his gravest, most serious voice.

Hardiman's frown deepened. "What history? I

thought Tenley confessed and took a guilty plea to avoid Old Sparky."

Chrys jumped in. "Yes sir, he did. But you might also recall he never named his client, the person who paid him twenty thousand dollars to murder Raina Noor."

Hardiman nodded as if it sounded familiar. "Why the sudden interest now, seven years after the murder, six years after the trial?"

"Raina Noor's husband was murdered last week. Same MO as Tenley. Someone broke into his house and bashed his skull in with a paperweight."

Hardiman grimaced. "Disgusting. Sounds like a copycat."

"Maybe. Or Tenley's mystery pal from seven years ago finishing the job."

Hardiman considered the theory, bobbing his head from side to side. "Could be. And you think the doer reached out to Tenley? For what—guidance, some killer to killer tips?"

"Could've," Burton responded.

Chrys' impatience had been building slowly, like a flame being stoked with oxygen. Burton had seen it out of the corner of his eye, sensed it in the energy crackling around her. He should have tamped it down when he'd had the chance. But he hadn't. And now, she erupted.

"Or to get some DNA to plant at the scene. That's right. Your golden boy's genetic material is all over the crime scene, warden. He's implicated in the murder. Maybe his old employer thought it would be funny to try to pin the husband's murder on the guy who was paid to kill the wife. I don't know. And we'll never know unless we get access to his communications. Is protecting your inmates' precious rights really more important than the public's safety?" she railed.

Hardiman was silent for a long moment. Burton watched his face and saw his eyes spark with understanding. Nine times out of ten, that would be a good thing, but something in the set of the warden's jaw told him this was number ten.

"You can't go to a judge with a subpoena. You'll get laughed out of the courtroom if you say Damon Tenley's a suspect in this new murder. Being incarcerated in a prison cell under 24-7 surveillance and supervision provides very few advantages to the inmate, but an airtight alibi for crimes committed on the outside is a big one. That's why you called me to see if he was present and accounted for after the murder. He was. So, you can't very well tell a judge you have reasonable cause because his DNA was at the scene. You won't get your subpoena, but you will get an outcry from the criminal defense bar, won't you?"

"I don't pretend to understand the way they think, Doug."

Hardiman wasn't fooled by the attempted sidestep.

"You and I both know they'll all be clamoring for new trials on account of unreliable work by the medical examiner's office. At a minimum, you'll have a massive headache on your hands. It might turn into a full-blown scandal. So you two thought you'd come out here and take a run at Tenley, see if he'd give up his partner. I don't fault you. It was worth trying. But it didn't work. And now you want me to violate his rights so you can try to shore up a new case while protecting the old one. Have I got that just about right?" He asked the question in a mildly curious tone, almost as if he were truly wondering.

But Burton wasn't fooled. He'd seen the steel glint behind those dorky glasses. "More or less."

Hardiman smiled. "They don't call me Hard Ass Man around here just because I expect the inmates to toe the line. I also hold my corrections officers and the rest of the law enforcement family to the same standard."

"Okay, maybe we overreached. How about you give us Tenley's list of approved telephone numbers? No recordings, no infringing on his private conversations. That's a fair compromise. We'll call it even."

"How about I don't tell Tenley he's got a cause of action against the commonwealth on account of the unreliable forensic evidence submitted at trial and we call that even."

The warden turned and stormed out of the visitors' room.

After a moment, Burton shrugged. "Let's retrieve our weapons and get out of this sewer. I want to get the stink off me."

Chrys arranged her features into a smile, but Burton could tell her heart wasn't in it. He couldn't blame her. After all, they'd just had their asses handed to them by a man wearing a sweater vest.

CHAPTER NINE

Damon lay on his metal bunk until his breathing returned to normal. It took a long time.

When he finally sat up, his head still swam. The gray walls blurred and spun. The coppery taste of fear filled his mouth. He jammed his hands under his thighs and sat on them so he wouldn't have to watch them shake and replayed the conversation with the homicide detectives.

Giles Noor was dead. Murdered.

Was he, though? The police were allowed to lie to a suspect—a fact that had always seemed like BS to him, but now carried dangers he couldn't quite untangle. This is what he got for not watching television or reading the news. He'd have to ask someone.

Assume it's true. The man was killed. They can't pin it on you, he assured himself. *You haven't been outside the barbed wire perimeter in over sixty-eight months. That's a good fact.*

His hands stilled under his legs.

It crossed his mind that the fact that he hadn't killed Giles Noor, while one hundred percent true, was not in any way helpful or relevant. There were enough guys in the joint who had pleaded guilty to crimes they hadn't committed for him to understand that factual innocence was irrelevant to the commonwealth.

His breath ticked up.

Come on, man, stay focused. Even if Noor's dead, they're probably not really trying to connect the murder to Raina's. They just see an advantage and they're playing it, hoping you'll give them a name so they can tie up loose ends from an old case.

Detectives were probably no different than platoon leaders or prison guards. They all liked order, hospital corners, and tidy explanations that ticked all the boxes. If they had any real leads on Noor's killer they'd be out chasing them down, not in here, leaning on him.

There was zero reason to think Giles Noor's death was connected to Raina's murder. Less than zero, actually. Still, though. There was only one way to know for sure.

He struggled to his feet, his knees bucking, and wobbled over to the bars that fronted his cage.

"Officer Smith?" he called.

A bald black pate swung toward the sound of his voice, catching the bright light and shining as if Rome Smith had an ethereal halo and not a run-of-the-mill chrome dome.

"You have a problem, Tenley?" the officer asked as he approached the cell, swinging his baton lazily against his thigh.

"I'm wondering if I could get a phone call, please? I know it's not my scheduled time, but I usually don't use my calls. Don't have anyone to talk to most weeks. But this is an emergency-type situation."

Damon made the request matter-of-factly, acknowledging that he was asking for a favor and stating the reality of his situation without playing for Smith's sympathy. It was all he could do. The result was in Smith's hands.

Smith twitched his nose from side to side like a rabbit. "You say it's an emergency? Like a family issue?"

"Something like that."

"You got money on your commissary account to pay for it? Or does this person accept collect calls from you?"

"Nah, no collect calls. I have money on the books. I probably still have pre-paid minutes available, too."

More twitching. This time the guard's lips joined in. Left, right, left, right.

"Okay. You're gonna get your call, Tenley. Wanna know why?"

"Yes, sir. And thank you, officer."

He holstered the baton and held up a massive hand to tick off points. "One, you said please. Two, you didn't try to bribe me with a half-smoked pack of cigarettes or some crumpled-up porno mag. Three, you don't cause trouble around here."

"Understood. And again, thank you. Also, it really is urgent."

"I don't give two craps about your personal situation. I just care that you're not making my job harder than it has to be, Tenley. I'll make the arrangements. Don't go anywhere." He made finger guns and grinned.

Like a good boy, Damon laughed at the jailhouse humor and squelched his irritation. He had to play nice. He needed to make this phone call. Someone's life might depend on it.

Damon breathed in through his nose, out through his mouth, the way the counselors taught him. He worked up some spit in his dry mouth, so he'd be able to croak out a greeting. Then he rolled his shoulders like a boxer entering the ring, shook out his wrists, and pressed the cold buttons with slow, hard jabs—depressing each number all the way down, waiting for it to lift, then pausing for a beat before moving on to the next digit.

When he'd entered all ten numbers, he gripped the phone to his ear and listened to the drumbeat of his heart while he waited for the line to ring.

He began to rehearse his words in his jumbled mind.

Sorry to call. Heard Giles Noor was killed. The detectives were here. They're going to try to pin it on you. That's crazy, right? Right? Don't worry, I didn't say anything. And I won't. But you need to be careful.

As long as he focused and managed to make each of these points, everything would be okay.

His hand cramped. He relaxed his grip and flexed his hand. Noise sounded in his ear, and he instinctively straightened up, ready to say hello.

But the phone wasn't ringing. Instead, a mechanical cacophony squawked in his ear. He winced and pulled the receiver away. A digital female voice informed him that the number he was trying to reach had been disconnected.

He stared down at the phone in his hand in disbelief. Disconnected. Unreachable. He'd been cut off.

Now what?

CHAPTER TEN

H ope sat cross-legged on the floor in Giles' study, surrounded by piles. Giles had been a saver. He kept user manuals, warranties, and receipts. He held on to copies of medical bills and service invoices. And, from the looks of one dangerously bulging accordion folder, every draft of his Ph.D. thesis, complete with a square diskette labeled "final version" clipped to the front of the folder. She was pretty sure finding a computer capable of reading the ancient diskette would require time travel.

The one saving grace was that in addition to being a packrat, he'd been organized. All the paper detritus of his life was sorted and categorized into neatly labeled folders, boxes, and files.

Thank the good Lord for small favors.

Even so, the prospect of going through all the documents made Hope's skin itch. She was the opposite of a saver. She moved through life with as little as possible, shedding papers, clothes, and belongings every step of the way.

Giles used to tease her about her extreme minimalism, but she'd brush off the comments with a light remark, saying she had her memories of experiences, so she had no need for ticket stubs, programs, and pictures. In truth, though, she scrubbed her memories with nearly as much vigor as she tackled her tangible possessions. Unpleasant or emotional memories were discarded like yesterday's newspaper.

At least she had the best ones. Giles' face lifted to the sun on an early spring day as they shared an impromptu picnic on the university's green. His fingers fumbling with the nest of pins securing her updo in the hotel room the night they were married. And the sharp intake of breath and yearning gleam in his eye when he removed the last pin and her hair tumbled in a cascade of blonde waves over her bare shoulders.

Tears welled up behind her eyes. Giles had cherished her in the truest sense of the word. He'd called her his second chance at love, at life, at happiness.

He never nagged her about leaving a glass in the sink or forgetting to take out the trash or running late. The petty domestic squabbles that erupted between the couples in their circle of friends were absent in their relationship. Losing Raina the way he had made Giles grateful for each day with Hope. He treated her gently, almost reverently.

And now he was gone in the ugliest way possible, and she was left to pick up the pieces.

Which is never going to happen if you spend the whole day dissolving into a puddle of tears on the floor, she chided herself.

Find the life insurance papers. Find the banking documents. Find the will. She knew these tasks, as mundane and soulless as they were, couldn't wait. That's why she'd forced herself to come into the study when she returned from her meeting with Detective Gilbert, even though she badly wanted to crawl into bed and shut out the world.

You can't.

When her father died years ago, after his cancer had metastasized to his bones, her mother had lapsed into a depression. Which was totally understandable, Hope knew. But the mortgage company hadn't been particularly sympathetic.

Mom missed one payment, the due date wiped from her mind by a wave of grief. Even though she sent the whole amount plus the late fee as soon as she'd realized her mistake, she'd ended up tangled up in a delinquency process that would have been complicated and tricky under the best of circumstances. As it was, Hope had spent hours on the phone, explaining the situation, swallowing her pride and begging for just a smidgeon of humanity while her mother stared helplessly at the stack of threatening letters.

Hope had to avoid a similar trap. Keep moving forward, keep what was left of her life running on autopilot as smoothly as she was able, until she cleared out the gray fuzz that clung to her brain.

A cloth-covered storage box labeled 'Insurance Papers' looked promising. She lifted the lid and set it aside. Then she walked her fingers through the row of manila folders, arranged in reverse chronological order. 2019, 2018, 2017. Her fingertips came to rest on a folder near the front of the box. A white label affixed to the folder tab read 'Hope—life insurance denial, 2016' in Giles cramped, legible printing.

Life insurance denial?

Her heart thudded in her chest. She was sure Giles had never mentioned applying for a policy on her life, let along having it rejected. Her throat constricted and her hands felt as if they were frozen, encased in ice.

After a long moment, she forced herself to remove the slim file from the box. She placed the folder over her knees and gingerly opened it, as if she feared a fire-cracker might go off. The file contained just two sheets of paper.

She skimmed the top document. It was a short letter, dated three months after their wedding date, and it informed Giles in terse, unapologetic language that his new wife was not qualified for the policy he'd chosen due to her 'preexisting medical condition.'

She flipped the page over and turned her attention to the second document. It was a sheet torn from Giles' notepad, dated just a few days after the letter. His hand-written notes memorialized a phone conversation he'd had with someone named Javier Morales, who worked in the insurance company's applications department. She scanned the summary. Giles had called asking for more information, certain there'd been some mistake. He'd written 'Hope is healthy' and had underlined healthy twice. Morales confirmed there was a HIPAA form on file from Hope's primary care physician and her pharmacist.

Had she consented to sharing her medical information with Giles?

She honestly couldn't remember. It seemed shocking now that she would have. But in the blissed-out glow of the first months of marriage, she'd probably seen no harm in doing so. They were a team. Giles and Hope. Husband and wife. No secrets.

Only, she'd had some secrets, after all.

Morales explained that the cyclosporine, the immunosuppressive medication she'd been taking, indicated a previous battle with either acute lymphoblastic leukemia or acute myeloid leukemia, either of which disqualified her from coverage under the plan Giles had chosen. Morales recommended a different plan, higher premiums, lower payout. Giles had dutifully printed the plan details on the sheet.

She could see where his pen had stopped. A blot of dark ink spreading under the word 'leukemia.' She imagined him sucking in his breath sharply, his hand frozen on the letter 'a' as his brain processed the news he'd received from a faceless stranger at an insurance company. Information his wife hadn't shared.

She closed the folder and sat motionless, staring at the bookshelf without seeing it. He'd known all this time about the leukemia and had never asked a single question. Never commented on her frequent doctor's appointments or on her occasional exhaustion, the times fatigue tackled her from out of nowhere and flattened her for a day or a weekend.

What else had he known?

She swayed to the side, lightheaded, and was

grateful she was already sitting. She set aside the folder and lowered herself to lie on her side on the floor. She pressed her cheek against the cool, smooth hardwood and closed her eyes. She wrapped her fingers through the knotted fringe of the area rug where she'd been sitting, pulling on the strands to stay grounded.

Her head buzzed. She focused on her breath. The buzzing continued, louder and more insistent. At last, she realized the sound wasn't in her head. It was her cell phone vibrating against the floor.

She struggled to sit up, still dizzy, and patted the piles of paper, searching for her phone. Finally, she unearthed it from under a stack of student papers Giles had been grading during his last night on earth.

"Hello?"

"Hello?"

The woman's voice was faint and wobbly. Bodhi could hear her labored breathing.

"Mrs. Noor?"

"Yes?"

"My name is Bodhi King. I'm a forensic pathologist

helping the medical examiner look into your husband's death. I'm sorry for your loss."

"Um, thank you."

"I know you must be incredibly busy, but I'd like to set up a time to chat, if you're willing."

"Chat?" Her voice was hesitant, almost wary. "I don't know anything about forensics. I'm not sure how I can help you."

"Why don't I just explain a little bit about what I do, and maybe it'll be clearer. I'm an independent consultant. I work mainly on thorny cases—cases that can't be explained using the standard procedures. As a result, I don't use standard methods. I just want to talk to you about your life with your husband. No science, I promise."

She wavered. "But ... I already talked to the detectives. I don't know what else I could tell you."

"I understand," he assured her in an easy tone. "But, I'm looking at the case from a different angle. Information that might not have seemed important to you or the homicide detectives could potentially help me find your husband's killer. I know that's what you want."

"Of course," she shot back instantly. "Why wouldn't I?"

Putting this woman on the defensive wasn't going to get him anywhere. He paused and smiled. Smiling imbued a communication with a friendliness that could be felt, if not seen, such as during a phone conversation. In fact, he often made it a point to arrange his expression into a smile when he typed an email. That's how convinced he was that it made a difference.

"I'm sorry. I didn't mean to imply otherwise. I do need your help, if it's not too much trouble. There are some ... unusual ... aspects to this case that I'm trying to work through."

Unusual was one way to put it.

"Oh, I see. You're trying to figure out why Damon Tenley's DNA was found at the scene, right?"

Bodhi fell silent. He stroked Eliza Doolittle's crown and wondered how Hope Noor knew the results of the DNA typing.

"Mr. King?"

Her quizzical voice shook him out of his thoughts. He stopped petting the bird, who head-butted his knuckles to express her displeasure.

"I'm here. I'm just surprised that the preliminary forensic results were shared with you. That's not typically done."

"Oh. Oh, no, I hope I haven't caused trouble for Detective Gilbert. He did tell me not to say anything to anyone. I just ... well, I assumed you already knew," she fretted.

"You were right on both counts, Mrs. Noor. I do know about the DNA results, and one of the knots I'm working to untangle is how the DNA results fit—or don't fit—with the rest of the forensic evidence."

As he reassured her, a warm rush of gratitude washed over him. He was glad the leak had come from the homicide squad rather than the medical examiner's office.

Then he frowned. Having an attachment to his former colleagues was dangerous. It could impede his work and lead to tunnel vision. He made a note to examine his emotions on the subject later.

"Oh, okay," Hope Noor exhaled audibly, her relief apparent.

"So, could I come see you sometime in the next day or two? Or we could meet at the medical examiner's office, but I thought perhaps you'd be more comfortable in your own home."

Whenever he could, he liked to conduct interviews on the witness's home turf. He had a few reasons for his preference. The first was just as he'd said: she'd be more at ease and, as a result, more apt to open up. The second was that environment was part of a person's larger essence. Being in the space where Giles and Hope Noor lived would create context and help him complete his picture of the dead man.

"I ... yes, I guess. Could you come tomorrow afternoon?"

"That would be great. Does 3:30 work?"

He could ride his bike to the Noor's Squirrel Hill home and then meander down the hill to Shadyside for his dinner with the David family, filling the time between commitments with a stop at his favorite used bookshop/tea shop. He'd have to remember to tell Saul he wouldn't need a lift after all.

"Yes, that's fine. You have the address?"

"I do. Thanks for agreeing to see me."

"Um, sure. I hope this doesn't turn out to be a waste of your time. Like I said, I've already told the police everything I know."

"You'd be surprised by how often seemingly irrelevant details end up being helpful," he told her.

"I guess so." Her voice was still filled with uncertainty and hesitation.

"I know so," he assured her before they ended the call.

CHAPTER ELEVEN

B odhi started his Thursday morning peacefully. Later, he'd be grateful for those first minutes of calm.

He stood on the small wooden deck just off the kitchen and watched the sun rise, pale orange in the crisp winter sky, with his hands wrapped around a steaming mug of tea.

Five hundred miles to the west, Bette would be watching the same sun poke its head up over the deep green trees that abutted her property. He breathed in the sharp, cold air and greeted the day and Bette under his breath.

When had he become so sentimental? He pondered the question as he finished his tea. After his chance encounter with Eliza last year, he decided.

Running into his medical school girlfriend, the woman whose heart he'd treated callously, had filed away the edges of some of his firmly held beliefs about nonattachment.

He shook his head, still slightly bemused, and headed inside. He should call Eliza and see how she and her boyfriend were doing. Funny how they both ended up involved with chiefs of police.

As he closed the door behind him, Eliza Doolittle squawked, "Phone call for Bodhi." She added a dead-on imitation of his cell phone ringtone for good measure.

"Thanks, Eliza Doolittle."

He gave the top of her head a few scratches and refilled her water before picking up his phone from the kitchen counter to check for a message.

He had two.

He pressed the speaker button and played the messages while he refilled the tea kettle with water from the sink.

Bette's throaty voice filled his kitchen:

"Morning. I'm watching the sun kick off its day and you popped into my mind. I was thinking I could leave Johansson in charge for the weekend and pop out to visit you. There's a discount flight to Pittsburgh from O'Hare tomorrow afternoon. I'd need to be back by midday Sunday. Let me know."

He considered the idea, a smile playing across his lips.

Then the second message began to play. It was from Saul, and his frantic tone was a stark contrast to Bette's easy drawl:

"Bodhi. It's Saul. When you're finished meditating or returning insects to the outdoors or whatever you're doing, get into the office as soon as you can. Someone leaked the DNA results to the media and Meghan's on the warpath. She's called a team meeting for eight o'clock."

He raised an eyebrow at the news and reached for the hard cake of fermented tea that Bhikkhu Sanjeev and Roshi Matsuo had pressed into his hands before he'd left Onatah. The aged *pu-erh* tea was a special gift in China, and the monks had thought it a fitting gesture to send him home with a disc after he'd solved the murder of a Chinese man on their retreat center's grounds.

Eliza Doolittle whistled. He paused in his tea preparations to turn and look at her. Her neck was bent at a sharp angle so she could eye him with one shining black eye.

"Bodhi's in trouble. Go to work. Call Bette. Big trouble."

He sighed. The macaw was intelligent and bossy. Living with her was like having an officious personal assistant. And he knew if he didn't respond, she'd just repeat her orders until he did.

"Thanks, Eliza Doolittle. I'm on it."

He took his mug and his phone and headed upstairs to shower.

First he returned Bette's call. He was disappointed but not surprised when the call rolled to her voicemail.

"Good morning, Bette. I was thinking about you while I watched the sunrise, too. I'd love for you to visit but this weekend might not be the best time. Someone just leaked investigation details to the local press, so ... well, I don't have to tell you. All hell's broken loose. If I had to guess, I'd say, we'll be scrambling all weekend to clean up the mess. But let's talk and figure out a time we can squeeze in a visit. I ... miss you."

The admission startled him even as he said the words.

He ended the call, took a long swallow of hot, earthy tea, and turned on the shower full blast.

Eight minutes and thirty seconds later, he was dressed and ready to go. He rinsed his mug and placed it in the kitchen sink and said goodbye to the macaw. Then he clicked his bike helmet strap closed under his chin and wheeled his bicycle out the door and down the stairs. He made a point to pause before he mounted the bike. He stood motionless and allowed the quiet and calm of the early morning to seep into his muscles and bones.

When the stillness settled into his chest, he swung his leg over the frame, adjusted his messenger bag across his chest, and began to pedal.

CHAPTER TWELVE

January 2013

The halls of the homicide squad were unusually hushed. The post-holiday lull in murders had been compounded by a bitter cold snap that was keeping people inside. Domestic violence calls were up, as cabin fever and boredom sparked flare-ups between family members trapped inside together. But, thankfully, none of those calls had escalated to murder.

Yet, Burton thought, as he trudged down the hall to the commander's office. *Give it time. Another week of sub-zero temperatures and arctic winds, and the tempers will reach a boiling point.*

He turned the corner and spied Chrysanthemum Martin loitering outside Commander Noonan's office. She shot him a look of dread as he neared her.

"You, too, huh?" He jerked his head toward the door.

"Yeah. You have any idea what this is about?"

He shook his head. "Nope."

That wasn't strictly true. There hadn't been any murders in the past several days, so they weren't about to catch a case. Which meant they were about to catch hell.

Noonan was a hands-off commander. He only interacted with the homicide detectives to assign them cases and ream them for transgressions, real and imagined.

From the expression on Chrys' face, she shared Burton's view of what lay on the other side of the door.

"Well, let's get it over with," she muttered as she raised a fist and rapped on the door.

As Noonan's hoarse voice shouted for them to come in, Burton reviewed the cases he'd worked with Chrys in recent months, wondering which one had landed them in hot water. He drew a blank.

Noonan filled it in before the door even closed behind them.

"Which one of you two's been running your mouth? Or is it both of you?" he demanded in lieu of a greeting.

Chrys shot Burton a wide-eyed look. He risked a small shrug, hoping it didn't catch the commander's notice.

He was as bewildered as she was, but he was also the senior detective, so he drew himself up straight and said, "Running our mouths about what, sir?"

Noonan slapped an open copy of the *Tribune-Review* down on his desk and pushed it toward them. "About the Noor woman's murder."

Crap.

Burton clasped his hands behind his back and leaned over the desk to read the headline that had gotten the commander's briefs in a twist: *"Squirrel Hill Slaying Not Random: Possible Personal Angle to Raina Noor Murder."*

Beside him, Chrys rocked forward to read it as well. She clicked her tongue in irritation.

"I don't talk to reporters, sir. I only mingle within my species," she said in a flat tone.

Burton caught the grudging glint of agreement in Noonan's hooded eyes. The commander's view of journalists as sub-human creatures wasn't exactly a secret around the squad.

"Whattabout you, Gilbert? You swallow your tongue?"

Burton gathered his thoughts. He hadn't leaked this

story. But he did hold a more charitable view of the fourth estate. He cultivated relationships with reporters the same way they developed their sources. He viewed it as no different from using a snitch, only reporters were usually not high or drunk and usually smelled better. Not always, but usually. He also sometimes used a friendly journalist to plant false information in an effort to shake the trees for fruit.

And everyone in the building, including the commander, knew it. A blanket denial would just enrage Noonan and convince the man that he had been the leaker, even though he hadn't.

So he met Noonan's eyes across the desk. "A below-the-fold piece in the metro section with a lame headline like that? In the Trib, no less? I don't mind saying I'm a bit offended. You'll know I've placed a story when you see a splashy, front-page, above the fold story in the *Post-Gazette* with a full-color photograph. Sir," he added belatedly.

Beside him, he sensed Chrys' sharp intake of breath. Noonan gaped at him. The clock on the wall ticked off impossibly long seconds. He forced himself not to fidget.

Finally, Noonan burst out laughing. He didn't stop until he was red-faced and wheezing.

"Go on, get out of here," he ordered, waving them to

the door as he wiped his streaming eyes and tried to catch his breath.

"Bold move," Chrys muttered from between her teeth as they scooted toward the door before he could change his mind.

The present

B urton glanced at Chrys' drawn, downturned lips.

"At least we don't have Noonan to deal with, like we did last time."

His attempt at making lemonade had no visible effect on her. If anything, the skin around her eyes grew tighter and the furrow carved into her forehead deepened.

"I think I'd take the commander over the district attorney." She spoke in a flat tone.

"She can rant and rave all she wants, but she can't bust us down to patrol. He could've—and would've—if he thought we had anything to do with this sh ... uh, circus."

'Circus' was putting it mildly. He had some better, more descriptive ways to communicate the mess someone had made of their investigation. But he recalled from the times they'd worked together that Chrys didn't care for cursing. So he tried to keep a lid on his swearing around her. Sometimes it even worked.

"Noonan never found out who leaked that story to the *Tribune-Review,* did he?" She slanted her eyes toward him.

"Not as far as I know. Why? You think the same joker called up Maisy Farley and spilled the details of the Giles Noor investigation?"

The perky blonde investigative reporter had solemnly informed viewers that, although no law enforcement officials had been willing to go on the record to comment on an ongoing investigation, she trusted her 'very connected' source to get the facts straight. It sure sounded like the leaker was on the team. Which meant this team meeting was going to be something special.

Chrys shrugged. "It's the most logical explanation. All I know is *I* haven't talked to any reporters."

"I know, Martin. You like to keep to your own species." He cracked a halfhearted grin and filled his lungs with air. "Come on, let's get it over with."

He pushed open the conference room door and they strode inside, shoulder to shoulder.

CHAPTER THIRTEEN

odhi glanced up when the door swung open. The homicide detectives burst into the room and whipped their heads around to take in their surroundings, twin glares on their faces. He half-expected one of them to shout 'All clear!' But they said nothing and slid into seats near the door.

The district attorney skipped the pleasantries this time. Not to mention the continental breakfast. Saul had said she was enraged by the leak, and it didn't seem to be an exaggeration. While they waited for the detectives, Bodhi, Saul, Tory, and Roland had sat in oppressive silence around the conference room table trying not to make eye contact with Meghan. Her expression was nothing short of murderous.

She glared around the table for a long, heavy moment. Then she threw her hands up into the air. "Well? Which one of you geniuses decided to give an exclusive to Maisy Farley?"

Nobody spoke.

"Don't all talk at once."

Roland Lee sighed. "Meghan?"

"What?" she forced out the words from between clenched teeth. "Don't even tell me that the leak came from our office, Roland. Do not. It was the new legal assistant, the one with the lip ring, wasn't it?"

"No. I mean ... I don't know if he or anyone else talked to the press. Although I really, really doubt it."

Roland paused, as if wondering whether another 'really' or two would convince his boss. Then he plowed forward.

"But I did call Annette."

"Morris?"

"Yes. I wanted to make sure I'm not missing anything or misremembering, so I pulled her notes from storage. You might not remember this, but she used a sort of shorthand of her own invention—"

"I remember."

"I needed to confirm some abbreviations. So, I called her."

Meghan grimaced. Then she nodded and said

slowly, "I can't imagine Annette maintained contacts at the local news stations after she moved. And I'm confident she wouldn't undermine our investigation by talking to the press. But, going forward, let me know before you contact her. "

"Understood."

Saul interjected. "I understand why you're upset, Meghan. And I agree the person who talked to the press made a mistake. But it's possible, maybe even likely, that he or she had good intentions." He spoke in the measured, reasonable tone of a man accustomed to dealing with small children.

Meghan narrowed her eyes. "Are you saying this leak came from your office, Saul?"

"No. I have no reason to think it did. I just want us to consider that the person who did share information you wanted to keep confidential may have had his or her reasons."

Meghan lifted one eyebrow and kept her attention locked on Saul. Bodhi wondered if Detective Gilbert was going to admit that he'd shared investigative details with Giles Noor's widow.

The detective must've felt Bodhi's eyes on him because he raised his head and met his gaze. He tilted his head to the side.

But the next person to speak up was Detective

Martin, not Gilbert.

"I told the warden when we went to Fayette."

All eyes turned toward Martin, who kept her expression blank.

Meghan scratched her neck and twisted her fingers around her chunky turquoise necklace. Then she shook her head. "Doug Hardiman doesn't strike me as the sort of person who would talk to the press. What's your assessment, Detective Gilbert?"

"I don't know Hardiman that well. But he seems like a straight shooter. If he did pass the information on to someone, I wouldn't expect it to be Maisy Farley."

His eyes flicked back to Bodhi.

Bodhi leaned forward and said, "I haven't talked about this case with anyone outside this room, but I do know Maisy. She's a friend. And I have spoken to her in the past about a case—when the energy drink death cluster situation came up."

He assumed most people in the room knew the broad strokes of that case and likely remembered that he'd sat for a televised interview to force Sonny's hand. It had worked, but he imagined his connection to Maisy landed him near the top of Meghan's list of current suspects.

"Could you talk to her now?" Detective Martin asked.

"Talk to ... Maisy?"

"If she's a friend, could you ask her who came to her?"

He shook his head. "I'm happy to try, but I'm sure she's not going to reveal her source. She takes journalistic ethics seriously."

"Give it a shot," Meghan instructed. Then she cleared her throat. "Okay, listen, I want to thank Roland and Chrys Martin for their honesty. And Dr. King, I appreciate your getting out in front of your relationship with Ms. Farley. Does anyone else have anything they'd like to share for the good of the order? Anyone else with friends in the media?" She aimed a meaningful look at Detective Gilbert.

He made a noise in the back of his throat. "The fact that I talk to journalists from time to time is an open secret. But I didn't tell Maisy or any other reporters about Damon Tenley's DNA turning up at Giles Noor's murder." His voice was serious and certain.

Bodhi tensed as he waited for the detective to go on.

"I did, however, share that information with Mrs. Noor yesterday morning."

Bodhi's shoulders relaxed. He'd hoped he wouldn't find himself in the position of having to rat out the homicide detective and was glad to avoid the issue.

Meghan frowned. "I realize that's your prerogative,

but I'm not sure that was the best idea, detective. We can't muzzle her."

"There's no way Hope Noor talked to a reporter. She doesn't want publicity, she wants closure. And she's smart enough to know shining a spotlight on the issue isn't going to help us solve her husband's murder any quicker."

"I hope you're right."

"I think he is," Bodhi chimed in. "I spoke to her yesterday, and she understood that she was to keep the details to herself."

"Why were you talking to her?" Detective Gilbert demanded.

"I was setting up a time to interview her."

"For what?"

"Giles Noor's autopsy was done before I got involved in this case. His corpse has already been buried. I can't use my usual investigatory methods, so I'm going to talk to the person who knew him best when he was alive."

From the skeptical twist of his lips, the detective didn't think much of Bodhi's fallback methods of investigation. Which, Bodhi had to admit, was fair. He didn't think much of them himself.

"I authorized the interview," Saul volunteered in a

patent attempt to shut down any objections. "And, as far as leaks from my office, I assure you there are none. Tory and I did discuss the results with an outside forensic testing lab because we want to get a confirmatory report from an independent entity, for what should be obvious reasons. But before we sent the samples, we required everyone at True-Type who would be handling the materials or accessing the case files to sign nondisclosure agreements. Tipping off the local press would be a violation of the NDA, exposing them to personal liability. And if we ever traced a leak back to a TrueType employee we'd terminate our relationship with the entire laboratory. It wasn't the lab."

"Besides, they weren't involved in the Raina Noor case," Tory added.

Meghan's smooth brow wrinkled. "Which is relevant why?"

"Don't you remember? There was a leak in the first Noor murder case, too. Someone told the press that Tenley committed the murder for hire. The police hadn't released the information about the shoebox full of money, but someone told a crime reporter at the *Tribune-Review*." She turned toward the detectives. "I'm remembering this correctly, right?"

"Yes," Detective Martin confirmed. "That's how it went down. In fact, Detective Gilbert and I were just talking about that leak on the way over here. We never found out where it came from."

"And you think this new leak came from the same source?" Meghan asked Tory.

"Sure. It stands to reason."

Meghan was silent for a long moment. She twisted a large garnet ring that she wore on the ring finger of her right hand. She exhaled a long *whoosh* of breath. "I don't plan to let this go, people. When I find the person who talked, there *will* be consequences. And if that person isn't in my agency, I'll be taking it up with Saul or the chief of police. *This will not stand.*"

Bodhi nudged Saul. "Are you going to tell her about Annette pressuring Tory during the first trial?" he asked under his breath.

"Not sure yet," Saul said in a low voice. "Why? You think that points to her being the source of the leaks?"

Bodhi shrugged. "It shows she plays fast and loose— or, at least, she used to."

"Hmm. Maybe."

He turned his attention back to the district attorney, expecting her to want the assembled group to provide updates. But, having vented her spleen, she waved a hand in a clear signal that they were dismissed.

"Go find Noor's killer."

As they filed out of the room, she sat immobile and

stared down at her notepad, the crease across her brow deepening.

CHAPTER FOURTEEN

D amon was working in the library, sitting on the floor, shelving some automobile mainte-nance and mechanic reference books on the low shelves, when Ronny poked his head into the room. He kept his body out in the hallway as if he didn't want to be caught setting foot inside.

Pretty weak, considering Ronny was writing a book of poetry. But Damon didn't call him out.

"Yo, Tenley."

Damon stood and stretched out his arm to give Ronny a fist bump. "What's up, man?"

"You tell me. You're the one on the TV."

"What?"

"You know that blonde lady reporter with the round butt and the juicy-looking boobs?"

"Maisy Something. Yeah." He wondered if she knew how many fans she had on Cell Block D.

"I was in Grayson's office getting some ... uh, help ... with a personal issue."

"And she just happened to be on, huh?"

"Yeah. Wild."

Grayson, the counselor, also a fan of Maisy Farley, was reluctant to turn off the news during the blonde's segments. And he seemed not to notice the steady traffic of inmates whose need for counseling coincided with her on-air appearances.

Damon shook his head. "You're not right, man."

Ronny shot him a grin. "Anyway, she was talking about you."

"Who was?"

"The blonde lady, man."

He frowned. "That can't be right."

"She says your DNA was found at a murder scene."

"Yeah, it was, but that's not news. It happened seven years ago. Maybe Grayson's been recording her segments and rewatching them for years or something."

Although that would be creepy. Even for Grayson.

Ronny laughed. "Nah, man. That chick you killed, somebody did her husband. But they left your DNA. Or else you got some hidden skills. You know how to get in and out of here, Houdini?"

Damon's stomach went sour, but he forced a laugh. "Yeah, right. If I was some kind of escape artist, you think I'd stick around here?"

"I dunno, it's a solid alibi. You know? I couldn't have killed that guy, your honor. I was in the joint."

Ronny had a point, but Damon hadn't been outside since he got locked up. No day pass, no court appearances, no emergency trips to the hospital. Nothing. So there was no way the cops found his DNA at a crime scene—that was if Professor Noor was even dead. Ronny was an okay guy, but he'd done a lot of meth. A lot. Maybe his brain was scrambled.

Yeah, Ronny's all screwed up. He's confused.

But the visit from the detectives yesterday kept forcing its way into Damon's brain. They *had* tried to get him to say he hated Noor. And if he had been offed, he wouldn't put it past them to try to pin it on him. Or to make up some story about his DNA to get him to flip and tell them who'd paid him to kill Raina Noor. They wouldn't care who they tagged with the kill, so long as they closed their case.

He laughed bitterly. Their read on him was all wrong if they thought he'd roll over to save his own hide. He was already in prison. Like Ronny said, he couldn't have done it. And even if they managed to convince a jury he had, what were they gonna do? He was here for life. Were they going to put him in double prison? Or maybe dig up his body after he died and send him back?

In the end it didn't matter whether Ronny was right or wrong. Nothing about his situation would change.

Having worked through all the angles, he nodded to himself and reached for the next book on his cart.

"Okay, Ronny. Thanks for telling me, I guess."

Ronny's eyes popped out of his head. He leaned across the threshold and slapped Damon right upside the head.

"Hey! What the—?"

"Don't be a dumbass. When I left the office, Grayson was handing me off to the CO and I heard him say something about you. The guard—that big, slack-mouthed dude from someplace in Europe, you know the one?"

"Vichevak."

"Yeah, him. He said Hardiman told O'Hagen that your lawyer will probably be able to get your sentence overturned now."

Damon's head snapped up. "For real?"

Ronny's eyes gleamed. "Yeah, for real, man. You gotta call your lawyer." He turned to leave.

"Hey, thanks, Ronny."

Ronny turned and thumped his fist against his chest. "Sure thing. You're cool, T."

Damon rocked back on his heels and dumped the

books back on the cart. He was halfway out the door, on his way to get his call set up, when he stopped short.

No. Shelve the books first. This is a long shot. If it doesn't pan out, you can't afford to piss off the librarian. Or the guards. Or anyone else.

He returned to the cart, scooped up an armload of books, and squatted alongside the shelf. He'd worked too hard to earn goodwill here to throw it all away on something that would probably turn out to be a big, fat nothing.

P enny Geoffries squinted at her computer screen and rubbed her temples with her fingertips. Her headache had been building all morning. All year, really.

She needed to get in to see her eye doctor to get bifocals. She knew it. She'd known it for months, ever since she'd been baking a batch of raspberry linzer hearts for her niece's wedding cookie table. The print on the recipe card she'd toted around for years—from dorm room to apartment to house—was suddenly illegible. Too small to read. Even if she'd stretched her arm way out and held it as far away as she could.

She'd called the next Monday for an appointment,

joking with the receptionist that she needed either bifocals or longer arms. But since then, she'd had to reschedule the appointment four different times. Budgetary cuts had left the Office of the Public Defender short-staffed. And Penny's caseload had ballooned accordingly, leaving no time for squeezing in optometry appointments. Or haircuts. Or a social life.

She sighed and pawed through the tower of papers and files on her desk until she unearthed the drugstore readers she'd tossed into her basket a few weekends ago when she'd run into the all-night pharmacy to pick up some more acetaminophen. As an afterthought, she dug the bottle of headache medicine out of the bag at her feet and shook two into her hand.

She was dry swallowing them when Kell Berg stuck his head through her open door.

"Did ya' hear?"

"Hear about what?" she asked her favorite investigator.

"Damon Tenley."

She searched her memory. "Killer for hire. Bludgeoned a young wife to death in Shadyside. No, Squirrel Hill. They got him on DNA and he took a deal. Life in prison rather than roll the dice and risk the death penalty."

Kell flashed an appreciative smile. "You still got it. Looks like he's about to get another roll of the dice."

She blinked. "How?"

"Maisy Farley on Channel 11 is reporting that a source close to the Giles Noor murder investigation claims Mr. Tenley's DNA was found at the scene."

"Noor. That name sounds familiar, but I haven't been following the news, Kell. I'm up to my elbows in work."

"Don't I know it. Giles Noor's name sounds familiar because he was married to Raina Noor, the woman Damon confessed to killing."

"And now he's dead?"

"He was bludgeoned to death last week in his Squirrel Hill home."

She shook her head, confused. "And the M.E. is saying they found Damon's DNA at the new murder scene? That's ... impossible. It's been, what? Five years?"

"Seven. And Saul David isn't saying squat. At least not for attribution. Farley didn't name her source."

Penny pushed the file she'd been working on to the side of her desk and leaned forward on her elbows, energized for the first time in months. She could feel the electric pulse of adrenaline coursing through her veins. "Do you have time to poke around to see if there's any truth to it? Because, if there is—"

"A 'Get Out of Jail Free' Card just fell into Damon Tenley's orange-jumpsuited lap," Kell finished excitedly. "I'll get right on it."

"Thanks. I'll have his files brought up from the archives in the meantime." She pulled a thick black notebook from her drawer. "His inmate number's in here somewhere. I'd better call him before he hears it on the block."

Kell nodded his agreement as her phone lit up. She raised one finger, asking him to wait, while she pressed the button to respond to the interoffice call.

"Penny Geoffries."

"Sorry to bother you Penny," one of the pool secretaries said, her voice tinny and distorted through the hands-free speaker. "An inmate call from SCI-Fayette just came in on the main line. This guy says you're his lawyer, but I don't see his name on any of your active files."

"Let me guess ... Damon Tenley?"

Kell raised an eyebrow.

"Girl, you're good. You oughta play the Powerball tonight!" The secretary laughed, and Penny knew it was Linda.

"Yep, he's mine, but his case file is inactive. Please put him through, Linda. Oh, and could you do me a favor and have his files sent up from storage?"

"You got it, Penny."

"Thanks."

She motioned for Kell to close the door and pull up a chair. Then she pressed the button to pick up the blinking line Linda had transferred. She was surprised to see her finger shaking.

"Hello, this is Penny Geoffries."

"Uh ... yeah, hi. This is ... my name is Damon Tenley. You're my lawyer. Or at least you were. Are you still my lawyer?"

The voice on the other end of the phone faltered, unsure.

"Yes, Mr. Tenley, I remember you. And even though your case is over, I continue to represent you for matters related to it. So, yes, I was your lawyer, and I *am* your lawyer." She infused her voice with as much warmth as she could dredge up from her exhausted being.

Her clients usually found the criminal trial process daunting and often thought the appeals process was incomprehensible. But this scenario had to be nothing short of bewildering.

"Oh, okay, good." He forced a nervous laugh.

"Before we go any further, I want you to know Kell Berg, my investigator, is in my office with me. He's listening to this call through my speaker phone. Is that okay with you?"

Kell leaned forward. "Hi, Damon."

Damon was silent for a beat, thinking. "He works for you?"

"Yes. So just like I am, he's bound by confidentiality rules not to tell anyone what you say."

"Uh, sure. Hi, Mr. Berg."

"Call me Kell."

"Kell, sure." Damon's voice slid into a question. "But my calls are being recorded, right?"

Penny twisted her mouth into a wry half-smile. "Inmates' personal calls are recorded by a contractor for the Department of Corrections, yes. Calls to counsel aren't *supposed* to be recorded ..." she trailed off. He'd been inside for six years. He'd catch the subtext.

"Right. So, the reason I'm calling ... did you see the news today?"

"Actually, Mr. Tenley, I haven't. But Kell was just filling me in on a possible development in your case."

"Yeah, I didn't see it either, but Ronny—uh, a fellow inmate—caught part of it in the counselor's office and, well, talk around here is maybe I can walk?"

She closed her eyes.

Jailhouse lawyers would be the death of her. When it wasn't the inmates themselves spouting half-baked legal theories, it was their friends and family. Or the corrections officers. Or social workers. Anyone with any

146

connection to someone within the penitentiary system seemed to think they'd earned a J.D. degree, without the hassle of three years of law school and passing the bar exam.

She breathed through her nose, exhaled, and opened her eyes.

"It's a bit early to make any promises or even to speculate. But if, in fact, the results of these recent forensic tests show your DNA at a new crime scene, they very well may call into question the reliability of the original results."

He fell silent as he processed her statement.

Kell cleared his throat. "In English, she's saying 'maybe, but don't get your hopes up.'"

Damon laughed. "Don't worry, I'm not. But what do we do now? Do you write a letter to the judge or something?"

"The first step is for me to contact the district attorney's office and request copies of these DNA tests. They ought to give them to me because they could exculpate you." She thought so, at least.

Probably. Maybe. It was complicated.

The whole thing was certain to be an unholy mess. Even if the DNA results proved to be contaminated, unreliable, or plain old wrong, they would be in uncharted territory. Just months ago, Damon would have been out of luck because he'd entered a guilty plea. But, back in October, the governor had signed legislation amending the commonwealth's Post-Conviction Relief Act.

One of the changes allowed convicts who'd pleaded guilty to access DNA testing results and to request testing when new forensic matching technology came on the market. Before the amendment, a defendant like Damon, who pleaded guilty couldn't seek DNA testing after conviction—even if the results would've exonerated him and overturned a wrongful conviction.

Penny thought it was long past time for the legislature to recognize the sad truth: a lot of defendants, especially those with limited resources, plead guilty to crimes they didn't commit rather than risk a longer or harsher sentence.

That said, Damon's situation was likely to be on the margins of the newly amended law. If the news report was accurate, new DNA testing would just as likely *inculpate* him in a second murder as it would exculpate him for Raina Noor's murder.

Of course, the second murder was one that he absolutely hadn't—and couldn't have—committed.

"Are you still there?" Damon asked.

"Yes. I'm just thinking it through. Maybe my first

step ought to be to talk to that reporter rather than the DA."

Kell blinked at her. "You want to talk to Maisy Farley?"

Penny nodded slowly. "I think so. The claim her source made doesn't only call into question the results of the forensic DNA testing in Damon's case—it casts a shadow on the results in *every case*."

Damon whistled, and Kell said something under his breath that she didn't catch. Penny had to hold back a laugh. Sometimes she envied the attorneys working in the prosecutor's office for their seemingly unlimited resources and the way juries and jurists seemed to believe every word they uttered in a courtroom.

But right now? She wouldn't switch places with Meghan Ford or one of her ADAs for anything. Not even for a week of solid sleep and a free afternoon to run errands and get new glasses. No way, no how.

Her laughter died on her lips. The mess about to hit the fan meant there was no way Meghan would be reasonable about Damon's situation. She couldn't afford to.

"Whatever you think is the best way to do this," Damon said. "What should I do in the meantime?"

"Keep your head down and your mouth shut," Kell advised.

"Absolutely. I know people will want to talk about it, just say your lawyer told you not to say anything for now." Penny added for emphasis.

"Okay."

"And Kell will come out to see you later this week. Probably Friday, once I've got a handle on the situation."

"Not you?"

She glanced at her desk calendar and the court appearances stacked one after the other.

"Not this week. Don't worry. Kell will be able to fill you in and answer any questions."

"Okay."

"But, seriously, Damon. Stay out of trouble, okay? Keep a very low profile."

"You don't have to worry about that. I know how to go along to get along. I wouldn't have lasted this long if I didn't."

"Fair enough. Take care and hold tight. We'll get some answers as soon as we can."

"Thank you."

"You're welcome, Damon."

"See you on Friday," Kell added.

She ended the call and leaned back in her chair. "Well?"

"Well, I noticed you didn't ask him to say he *didn't* manage to kill Giles Noor."

She pulled a face. "Come on, Kell. You know you never ask them if they did it."

"Surely you can when they *couldn't* have."

She shrugged. "Blanket policy."

"What about Raina?"

"What about her?"

"Did he kill her?"

She frowned. "What kind of question is that?"

"I'm just trying to think like a prosecutor. Even if their DNA evidence is total crap, he did have an envelope full of money—"

"I'm aware of the facts."

"—with *Payment for Noor job* written on it."

"Kell, I know. But, actually, it was a shoe box, not an envelope. And don't forget the towel from the Noors' bathroom he had stuffed under the floorboard with the box."

Kell chuckled. "I forgot about the hand towel."

"Yeah, well, neither the money nor the towel would've been admissible at trial. And they won't be admissible now, either."

"You're kidding."

"Nope. The police conducted an illegal search."

"So the evidence is fruit of the poisonous tree?"

"Close. It's actually covered by the exclusionary doctrine. But it's the same idea: the police didn't have the right to search Damon Tenley's home. They only had an arrest warrant. So anything that wasn't in plain sight, which includes that money, is excluded from evidence. I always figured that was why they didn't try harder to find the person who paid him. With the box excluded from evidence and without Damon's testimony, they'd be hard-pressed to make a case. You know?"

Kell whistled, long and low. "Yeah, Meghan's not going to let this go without one heck of a fight. Starting with the reporter's the right call."

She sighed. It was. She just needed to wring an extra hour out of her day somehow to make it happen.

CHAPTER FIFTEEN

M aisy was wiping away her thick camera-
ready mascara with a cotton ball soaked
in micellar water when her cell phone
chirped. She ignored it and kept working on her makeup
removal.

The blooming phone had been blowing up for hours.
Judging by her message log, the calls had started pouring
in before the segment had even finished airing. The
impossibility of an incarcerated man leaving his DNA at
a crime scene had stirred something in the viewing
public—the terrifying specter of science run amok
captured their imaginations.

She paused the circular motions and lifted the
cotton ball, now streaked with black, to give herself a
rueful look in the lighted magnifying mirror.

Fine, she amended, *the impossibility of it and the vicious irony of Giles Noor's murder.*

Noor's brutal killing was a ghoulish reenactment of his beloved wife's murder years earlier. She couldn't pretend the creepy fascination factor didn't play a role in the way the story had landed. Despite her efforts to frame the segment as the serious news piece it was, it *did* have a strong Nancy Grace vibe.

In fact, she wouldn't be surprised if a national cable show called her. Maybe even Nancy herself.

The door to the cramped dressing room creaked open and Julian, her producer, appeared in the doorway with his hands covering his eyes. "Are you decent?"

"Why, sugar? That boyfriend of yours afraid I'm gonna turn you straight?" she joked into the mirror. "Yes, it's safe. I'm fully clothed."

He laughed and lowered his hand. "Great piece this morning, Maisy. Really great."

"Thanks. It seems to be resonating. My phone's been ringing like crazy."

"Yeah, the station phone, too. That's why I'm here." He waved a fistful of phone messages at her. "These are purported tips. Most of them are crackpots. But you never know ..."

She held out her hand, palm up. "Give 'em here, and

I'll run 'em down. Could find a gem among the alien abduction and lizard man conspiracy theories."

"Want me to have an intern take the first cut, cull out the clear losers?"

"Nah. I'll do it. It'll keep me off the streets and out of trouble." She winked, and he handed over the stack of papers.

"Maisy, darling, I don't think you're capable of staying out of trouble."

She flapped her free hand at him. "Look at you, sweet talker. Flattery'll get you *everywhere*." She batted her eyelashes.

He guffawed.

They wore their shtick like a pair of comfortable slippers. She adored Julian. And the fact that their jokey, innuendo-laden repertoire drove everyone else at the station bananas was just a bonus.

After a long moment, his smile faded and he put on his serious journalist face. "We should work on a follow-up story right away while you have momentum. What do you think about a sit down with the widow?"

"Mmm. I'm not sure. It seems a little intrusive this soon after her husband's death, don't you think?"

"Maybe. But it would be a great ratings draw. The mourning young wife always is."

"Yeah." She tried the idea on for size and gave it a

minute to see how it felt. Then she shook her head. "I don't think so, honeybun."

He twitched his lips, thinking. "How about the murderer?"

She dropped the cotton ball on the vanity as a rush of energy coursed through her. Forget Nancy Grace and her podcast, *Primetime Justice* would probably want this story. Or maybe even Marcia Clark.

"Sit down for a prison exclusive with Damon Tenley? In a hot minute."

Julian grinned. "That's my girl. I'll call Doug Hardiman, the warden out there, and see what I can do."

"In the meantime, I'll get cracking on the tinfoil hat brigade." She fanned out a handful of the messages.

Julian dropped a kiss on the crown of her head and left, pulling the door shut behind him. As his laughter trailed him down the hallway, her eyes fell on the fourth message in her fan: *Annette Morris has information about the Raina Noor case.*

Annette Morris. The name niggled at the edge of her memory. Before she could access her mental Rolodex and place the woman, her cell phone rang again. She checked her display: *Bodhi.*

She swiped to answer the call.

"Bodhi King, isn't this a nice surprise. How's my favorite Buddhist?"

"I'm well, Maisy. You?"

His voice, as always, reminded her of a cool waterfall.

"Busy as a queen bee, and twice as bossy."

"Buzzy as a bee too. All anyone can talk about around here is the report you aired today."

She smiled, satisfied. "Around here? You're back in town?"

She'd heard he was spending time in some postage-stamp Midwestern hamlet, mooning over its chief of police. As if Pittsburgh could afford to lose such an eligible bachelor to corn country. She pushed out her lower lip in a pout even though the effect would be lost over the phone.

"I'm back, and I'm consulting on a matter for the medical examiner's office."

"Ooooh. Really? Would it happen to be the Giles Noor murder?"

"As a matter of fact, it would."

"Let me guess. You want to know who my source is on the DNA story? Now, Bodhi, you know I don't kiss and tell."

He laughed throatily. "Same old Maisy, I see. I wouldn't ask you to do that. But I do have a proposition for you. A business proposition," he added hurriedly.

"Hmmph. That's disappointing ... but fine. What do you have in mind?"

"Why don't we sit down, and I can answer any questions you might have about the medical examiner's forensic testing procedures. I won't comment on any specific cases, but I think you'll find the background information helpful."

She tilted her head to the side while she considered it. He was right. It would be useful to have a better understanding of the science. "And in return?"

"Nothing. It'll be a benefit to the office and the case if you have solid information. That's all."

With anyone else, her antenna would be up. But this was Bodhi. He didn't have the capacity to be dishonest or manipulative. And she'd love to see him again. For all her over-the-top flirting, she considered him a friend.

"Okay, yeah. That would be great."

"Fantastic. I have a meeting in Squirrel Hill this afternoon, and then I'm having dinner with Saul. Can we get together for an hour in between? Say around 5?"

"Sure. I'm getting ready to leave for the day. Why don't you stop by my building after your meeting and we can walk somewhere nearby for coffee or something?"

"You're still at the same place—that loft in Shadyside?"

"That's the one."

"I'll see you at five."

"I'm looking forward to it," she said. She ended the call and checked her face for any remaining traces of makeup. Satisfied, she swept the stack of messages into her oversized purse, turned out the lights, and left the dressing room, shrugging into her coat.

She wrapped her long deep purple scarf around her neck, letting the ends flutter behind her as she strode down the hallway, her heeled boots clicking against the tile floor.

She was waiting for the elevator when her phone rang again. She plucked it from her pocket. She didn't recognize the caller's phone number, but anyone who had her cell phone number was either a friend or a source who'd proved himself or herself to be valuable. Everyone else had to go through the station.

"This is Maisy," she trilled.

"Hi, Maisy. It's Penelope Geoffries from the public defender's office. I'm not sure if you remember me, but we—"

"We co-chaired the Big Sister luncheon last year. Of course I remember you, Penny. How've you been, darlin' girl?"

"Good, good. I'm calling about your segment this morning on the news."

"Yes?"

"Damon Tenley was—is—my client."

A bell chimed, announcing the arrival of the elevator car. The doors slid open. Maisy scrunched up her face apologetically and shook her head, pointing to the phone at her ear. The occupants of the car seemed unfazed.

She waited until the doors closed and the elevator continued its descent to the lobby. Then she said, in a calm voice that belied her racing pulse, "You represented him in the Raina Noor murder case?"

"Yes. I also represent him with regard to the claim that he's a match for any genetic material found at the Giles Noor murder scene."

"I see," Maisy said carefully.

"I'd love to talk to you about the DNA situation."

"I'd love to hear what you have to say. In fact, my producer is trying to arrange an interview with Mr. Tenley, so he can tell the public his story himself. Do you think he'd be interested?"

"Hmm. Yes, he might. I'll talk to him about it. Could you and I get together and go over the specifics? You know, what topics and questions would be off-limits ... that type of thing?"

Maisy wetted her lips with the tip of her tongue then stifled a laugh. She was glad Penny couldn't see how eager she was, how badly she wanted this sit down with her client. "That'd be great. When do you want to talk?"

"Well ... we're starting our own investigation now, and things will start to happen pretty quickly if we determine Mr. Tenley's eligible for post-conviction relief. So, the sooner the better. If we file a petition under the PCRA, we'll need to shift our focus to litigation, not public relations."

"Sure. And the PCRA is, what, exactly?"

"Sorry, the Post-Conviction Relief Act."

"Wait. Are you saying Damon Tenley's not guilty of murdering Raina Noor?"

"No, I'm saying he may have been wrongfully convicted of murdering Raina Noor."

"Are those the same thing?"

"Not even a little bit."

Maisy frowned. She had a good friend who practiced law. Maybe she'd have to convince Sasha to give her a quick lesson about wrongful conviction. In the meantime, she didn't want to lose Penny. Time to reel her in.

"Are you available this afternoon? I could meet you at four o'clock at the Book Seller/Tea Cellar right off Walnut. Do you know it?"

"I am, and I do. I'll see you there."

"Great."

Maisy stowed her phone back in her pocket and laughed. Her day just kept getting better and better.

CHAPTER SIXTEEN

Burton's day just kept getting worse and worse. Every path he started down ended with him smacking his face against a metaphorical brick wall.

He'd pulled the old interviews from the Raina Noor murder and had combed through them, scouring them for any hint about how Damon Tenley could have crossed paths with her before the day he ended her life. He found nothing. Nobody knew anything.

He shifted in his chair and pushed the interviews aside to turn to the copy of Tenley's service record the Department of Defense had sent over during the original investigation.

Tenley had apparently been spurred to join the military after the September 11 attack. On October 7,

2001, the same day the United States invaded Afghanistan and launched Operation Enduring Freedom, Damon Tenley, then age seventeen, presented himself at the Army recruitment office in Monroeville Mall with his guardian, who consented to his deferred enlistment.

After graduating from high school the following June, Tenley reported for ten weeks of basic training in Fort Still, Oklahoma, followed by fourteen weeks of infantry unit training. By October of 2002, he was overseas, fighting insurgent forces in southern Afghanistan's Helmand Province.

His service record was devoid of anything noteworthy—good or bad. Apparently, Infantryman Tenley kept his head down, followed orders, and managed to stay alive through two long deployments. There was no evidence his behavior ran afoul of any military code of conduct or civilian laws when stationed stateside in Georgia. He served five years active duty, and three years in the reserves. On October 7, 2009, Tenley extended his enlistment for a term of three years to take advantage of a stop-loss bonus and returned to active duty.

On October 31, 2012, Tenley separated from the Army in Fort Benning, Georgia, with an honorable discharge and returned to Pittsburgh to pursue a career in computer programming. Twenty-nine days later, Raina Noor was dead.

Burton frowned at the dry summary of utterly useless information.

Chrys rapped on the doorframe. He glared up at her.

"Tell me something good. Please."

"You asked for it, you got it. I found an army buddy of Tenley's. His name is Van Lewis. He manages a bowling alley in Lawrenceville, and he's willing to talk to us."

"You're a rock star, Chrys."

"I know." She shot him a grin.

"Seriously, you are. These files are useless. According to them, Damon Tenley was a regular G.I. Joe. I was beginning to think we were going to have to drag our butts down to Fort Benning to get any real insights." He stood up and turned out his desk lamp.

She wrinkled her nose. "Georgia? Uh-uh, no thank you. I don't like the heat."

"It's the dead of winter, Martin. But it doesn't matter, let's start with Mr. Lewis and maybe we'll hit a strike."

Another nose wrinkle. "Your puns are terrible. You know that, right?"

"Deal with it. It's how I roll." He mimed rolling a bowling ball.

She groaned dramatically and dangled the keys from her fingers. "Just for that, you're driving."

Chrys refused to be intimidated by his size, gruffness, and generally cranky attitude. It was one of his favorite things about her. He preferred working alone, always. But partnering with Martin was a distant second choice.

He snagged the keys from her hand and grabbed his overcoat.

As they headed down to the car, he said, "How'd you find this guy anyway?"

"Well, seeing as how Hardiman hasn't coughed up Tenley's visitors list yet, I took a flier. I called up a friend at the county jail and asked whether Tenley had any visitors while he was there. Mr. Lewis came to see him twice."

Good old-fashioned detective work. No high-tech forensics lab, no computerized programs to sniff out social media posts or read email or whatever the geeks in the technology unit did all day. She used her brain and a telephone.

"Good work, Chrys." They stepped out into the lot and he turned his collar up against the wind.

She tried, and failed, to hide a smile. "We'll see if it pans out."

"Was Van Lewis Tenley's only visitor?"

"Yeah. So, keep your fingers crossed that he's a talker."

V an Lewis eyed the pair of detectives across the counter as he reached for a pair of rental shoes a bowler was returning.

"I don't understand why the police want to talk about Damon now. He's been in prison for years."

Burton forced a smile. "Sure. But his name's come up in the course of a new investigation, and we just need to rule out his involvement."

Lewis squinted at him from behind a pair of dirty glasses. "We can talk in the party room. My office is the size of a closet and, wouldn't you know, doubles as a supply closet. So unless you wanna sit on an overturned mop bucket—"

"The party room'll be great," Chrys assured him.

"Kayla, take over the rental counter," he called over in a loud voice that was barely audible over the din of balls thwacking the pins, pins clattering to the ground, and electronic beeps, whirrs, and dings. Somehow the girl wheeling a cart of bowling balls toward the end of the room heard him. She raised a hand in acknowledgment.

Burton's temples thumped and pulsed with pain. He'd been in here all of four minutes, and he already had a headache. How did these people work here?

"Sorry about the noise," Lewis shouted. "You guys want a pop or something?" He gestured toward the soda machine.

"It's nice of you to offer, but we're good. We don't want to take up any more of your time than necessary," Chrys said.

Burton nodded his agreement using the smallest possible head movement.

Lewis ushered them to a glassed-in, rectangular room that housed a long cafeteria table and a dozen or so metal chairs. He flicked on the lights and closed the door behind them, muffling the noise.

"It's quieter in here than in my office, too," he said in a low, resigned voice. He looked from Burton to Chrys. "Does it matter where I sit?"

"Nope," Burton told him. "Sit anywhere you like. Like Detective Martin said, we'll try to make this quick. Thanks for meeting with us."

Lewis deposited himself into the nearest seat. "No problem."

Burton and Chrys pulled out two chairs directly across the table, and Chrys flipped open her notebook.

"You and Damon were in the same infantry company?"

"Yeah."

Burton recognized the shadow that crossed the man's face. He'd seen the expression countless times on everyone from Korean War vets to young guys just back from the Middle East.

"Thank you for your service," Chrys said, managing to infuse the tired, trite words with feeling and sincerity.

Lewis shrugged it off, but his eyes lightened.

"Would you say you were good buddies?"

Another shrug. "Good enough. We were in the same bunk house. We were both from Pittsburgh. He lived up the hill from here, in Stanton Heights. I grew up right across the river in Sharpsburg. So we had that in common. We talked about the Steelers, mostly. He was a good guy, solid guy."

"Damon re-upped when his initial term of service expired. Did you?"

"Nah, man. I wasn't one of those young guns like Damon, all pumped up about being a soldier. I went in under one of those programs to boost enrollment, Call to Service or something like that? I got an enlistment bonus and only served twenty-four months on active duty. The rest of my time was in the reserves. I got a business degree on Uncle Sam's dime out of the deal, too."

"But you and Damon stayed in touch?"

He lifted a shoulder. "I guess. When he came home on leave, we'd have a beer or two. And when he got discharged and decided to come back here for good, I told him he could work here until he figured out what he wanted to do."

"Did he take you up on that?"

Tenley hadn't mentioned a job during his interviews. Burton wondered if Lewis had been paying his buddy under the table.

"He didn't get the chance. He wasn't even back a month when ... you know ... that lady was killed."

Burton cocked his head. "You think he didn't do it?"

"I don't know. I was surprised when he got arrested, right? Obviously, he's killed people. We were infantry. That was our *job*, you know? But I never figured Damon for a psycho. Some guys got off on it. You could tell. Not Damon. So, I just couldn't—can't—see him whacking some random lady."

"He got paid, though. Twenty thousand dollars is a nice start to civilian life," Chrys observed.

Lewis shook his head. "He had money socked away from all those years in the Army with no living expenses. His parents' cancer treatments ate up what money they had, so they didn't leave him an inheritance or anything like that. But he had their house. And a job, if he wanted it. He didn't need to do it for the money."

The guy had a point. Burton switched gears. "You have any idea what he did for the month of November?"

Lewis thought for a moment. Chrys doodled a snowflake on her notepad. Burton resisted the urge to massage his temples.

"After he got out of the hospital, you mean?"

Chrys' pen stopped mid-flake. Burton lowered his chin and looked at Lewis over the tops of his glasses. The shift in attention levels must've made the bowling alley manager nervous. He took off his own smudged glasses and rubbed the hem of his shirt over the lenses.

"What happened? Do you know why he was in the hospital?" Burton asked in the most casual tone he could manage.

"Uh ... not really. All I remember is I called him up to see if he wanted to get some wings and beers and watch the game one Sunday, and he said he couldn't. He was going in for some kind of procedure and had to fast. I asked if he needed a ride. He said no, but he asked if I could stop by his place and bring in his mail for a few days."

"Did you?"

"Yeah. He didn't get any mail, really. Just junk. He'd

only been living at his parents' place for maybe a week. Most of it was still addressed to them."

"And you don't have any idea what was wrong with him?" Chrys pressed him.

"No. I figured it was his personal business. I didn't want to pry." He returned his glasses to his face and gave Chrys a puzzled look. "His sister might know. They were pretty tight."

CHAPTER SEVENTEEN

Bodhi carried his bicycle up the cement stairs to Hope Noor's front porch, where he lowered it from his shoulder and rested it against a wrought-iron glider. He turned to smile and wave at the woman across the street. She stood on her toes, clutching her sweater closed with one hand, while she ostensibly checked her mailbox for the day's mail. He was pretty sure she was actually just keeping an eye on her neighbor.

She blinked, caught in the act, raised a fistful of advertisements, and returned the wave.

He tucked his bike helmet under his arm and raised his hand to lift the door knocker but, before he had the chance, the door swung open to reveal a pale woman. Her blonde hair was piled on the crown of her head in a loose knot. She wore a long cardigan sweater over jeans and a black turtleneck. The dark color near her neck accentuated the circles under her eyes. A stab of compassion tore through his chest. She looked over his shoulder and frowned at her nosy neighbor.

"Hi, Mrs. Remmy," she called.

Bodhi turned in time to see the woman duck inside her house and pull the door closed. He turned back to the woman in front of him.

"Mrs. Noor?"

"Yes, are you …?" She trailed off, her eyes shifting uncertainly from his mop of curly hair to the bicycle propped against her porch furniture. "Um, are you with Mr. King?"

"I'm Bodhi King." He smiled and dug an old business card out of his wallet. He handed it over for her to inspect.

She raised her eyes from the card with a horrified expression. "I'm sorry, Dr. King. I didn't realize you were an M.D. And … I shouldn't have assumed you weren't you." She flushed a deep red.

He shook his head and gave her an easy smile. "Please, don't apologize. You couldn't have expected me to look like this." He stretched out one arm, gesturing to include his appearance and his preferred mode of transportation. "And I don't put much stock in titles."

She smiled politely and tucked the card into her cardigan pocket. "Still, I should know better. Please, come in."

"Thanks." He paused inside the door to wipe his feet on the mat. "Do you mind if I take off my shoes?"

"Um ... no?"

"Great." He slipped off his shoes while she closed and locked the door, then he padded after her in his stocking feet as she led the way to a casual family room where a fire burned in a gas fireplace.

"I thought we'd talk in here?" She hesitated in the doorway.

"Sure. Wherever you'll be most comfortable, Mrs. Noor."

"Please, call me Hope."

"Okay, Hope."

"I'd like to talk here. I've been spending a lot of time in this room lately. ... I don't like being upstairs alone." She shivered and wrapped her cardigan around her torso.

"Of course."

He waited for her to choose a seat first. She took the armchair next to the fireplace, so he sat across from her. She'd barely settled in, folding her legs up under her on the chair, when she suddenly popped back to her feet. "I'm sorry. Can I get you a drink?"

"That's very kind of you, but I don't need anything."

She returned to her seat and folded herself into a tight pretzel, with her legs tucked up under her and her arms crossed low over her lap. "I noticed on your card that you work for the medical examiner. I thought you said on the phone that you were an independent consultant?"

"I am. But I don't have any current business cards handy, and I figured you'd want to confirm my identity."

She nodded, accepting the explanation. "So you used to work for the Allegheny County Medical Examiner?"

"Yes, several years ago." He paused for a moment to consider what he was about to say, then added, "I was working there when your husband's first wife died. I performed Raina Noor's autopsy."

"Oh," she breathed. She squeezed her eyes shut, the skin at the corners wrinkling from the tension.

He waited until she exhaled and opened her eyes. When she focused on him again, he said, "The circumstances of your husband's death must be doubly shocking in light of what happened here seven years ago."

She swallowed. "Yes, you could say that. I mean, I didn't know Giles well back then. And I'd only met Raina once or twice ... but, of course, she—or at least her death—was almost like the third person in our marriage."

"How so?"

She twisted to her side and watched the flames dancing in her fireplace while she answered his question in a soft voice. "Giles was a mess after Raina died. She was his whole world. I was working in the history department as an administrative assistant while I was getting my degree, and he sort of fell apart. I felt so sorry for him. We grew close, but he was still mourning Raina's death when we started dating. I sometimes … wonder … if he ever truly moved past it."

"Grief can be a lifelong companion. But that reality doesn't detract from what you had with your husband."

She turned to face him. Tears shone in her eyes, threatening to spill out. She scrubbed her hands over her face and took several deep breaths. "You're right. I mean, I know that, intellectually. I'm so emotional these days."

"Of course you are."

"It doesn't help that we argued the evening Giles died."

"Do you want to talk about it?"

"It was so silly. Just one of those dumb arguments that married couples have now and then. But I was so irritated with him. And before I left for yoga, I made this crappy remark to him about living in the past. And when

I came home, he was ... gone." She was crying freely now, making little hiccupping sounds as she sobbed.

He crossed the room and crouched beside her chair. He dropped a hand on hers and made a soothing, shushing sound. After a moment, she raised her head again.

"Sorry."

"You have nothing to be sorry about. You're grieving. You should be as gentle with yourself as you were with Giles after Raina died."

She attempted to smile. "Thanks," she whispered.

"Of course. And I'm sure your husband knew you loved him." He withdrew his hand gently and returned to his seat.

He knew he risked compromising his objectivity if he focused on the woman's strong emotions, but he couldn't ignore her pain. She seemed impossibly frail—like an injured sparrow or a delicate glass that threatened to shatter.

She made a high, strangled mewling sound and pushed herself out of the chair as he began to walk away. "Will you excuse me for a moment? I just need to splash some water on my face and pull myself together."

"Absolutely. Take your time."

She nodded and darted from the room.

Hope patted her face dry with a hand towel then checked her reflection in the mirror. She looked like death warmed over. She yanked the elastic hairband from her hair and shook her hair loose so it hung over her shoulders.

Now she looked worse. She raked her fingers through her hair in an attempt to coax the jumble into orderly waves. It was no use. She hurriedly swept it back up into a knot and secured it with the band.

Keep it together. He's not even remotely intimidating or scary. There's no reason to fall apart. Just answer his questions and he'll be on his way.

She nodded at her own instructions, watching her reflection in the mirror.

She never should've brought up the fight. It had stirred up too many feelings. She'd panicked, though, when she saw Mrs. Remmy watching her receive a visitor. Mrs. Remmy was a thoughtful neighbor, and she'd been very kind over the past week. But everybody on the block knew she was an unapologetic busybody.

Hope and Giles used to laugh at her nosiness. Giles called her 'Nebby Nellie.' She wasn't even sure her first name was Nellie.

Hope knew Mrs. Remmy had heard their fight last

Tuesday. When she'd woken up in the Remmys' guest room the morning after, she'd overheard Mrs. Remmy telling her husband that Hope had been shrieking at Giles 'like a caterwauling alley cat.'

The last thing she wanted was for Mrs. Remmy to waylay Dr. King when he left and fill his head with stories that made it sound as if she and Giles had had a troubled marriage. Or that made her seem like some sort of shrew. For reasons Hope couldn't quite articulate, even to herself, it mattered what the kind-eyed forensic consultant thought of her. And of Giles.

She pinched her cheeks to add a hint of color to her washed-out complexion. Then she took one last look at herself, threw back her shoulders, and walked out of the powder room as calmly as she could.

When she returned to the family room, Dr. King was standing with his hands clasped together behind his back, inspecting the titles of the books that lined the floor-to-ceiling bookcases on each side of the fireplace.

B odhi heard Hope Noor's light footfalls on the hardwood in the hallway and turned when she reached the doorway to the room.

"Are you feeling better?"

"I am. Thank you." She nodded.

"You have an interesting collection." He gestured toward the bookshelves.

"Oh, I guess. Most of the nonfiction down here is mine. Giles keeps—kept—his reference materials, biographies and histories, that sort of thing, in his office upstairs. The fiction titles are a mix. Some are mine, some are his."

"I see you have a copy of the Chumash. That's the text of the Hebrew Torah, isn't it?" She came to stand beside him and looked at the volume as if she'd never seen it before.

"Yes, that belonged to Giles. He wasn't always religious—I think I've explained this to Dr. David already, so I'm sorry if I'm repeating myself ...."

"No worries." He waved a hand to indicate she should continue.

"Okay, well, his family was Sephardic, from Spain. And they always identified more as Spaniards than as Jews. I mean, he didn't grow up really practicing any faith."

"Sure."

"But, after Raina's death, he was floundering, I guess you'd say. Over the years, he tried out a couple different synagogues, some churches, even a Quaker meeting. Finally, he decided he felt comfortable at a progressive congregation just down the street. He wasn't ever particularly devout, but it did matter to him. So, I thought I should honor his beliefs in death."

"Does Giles have any close relatives? A parent or a sibling, for instance?"

She shook her head. "Neither of us do. His parents were much older when he was born. They both passed away when he was in college. And mine did, too, actually. I was a freshman when Dad's cancer took him. My mother was dead a year later. Maybe that's why Giles and I were drawn to each other." Her lower lip shook, and she clamped her front teeth down on it.

"I'm sure you were a great comfort to one another."

She looked at him with a slight wrinkle across her brow. "Dr. King, I don't want to seem rude, but how does any of this help you determine how Damon Tenley's DNA showed up in the forensic testing results?"

It was a fair question, so he gave it a fair answer. "I'm not sure it will. When I worked as a medical examiner, my job was fairly straightforward. The deceased body told me his—or her—story. But, as a rule, I don't perform autopsies anymore. So, I try to piece that story together from disparate parts of the victim's life. Sometimes a fear or a passion they had in life will shine a light on how or why they died. I'm sure that sounds vague and not very reliable, but it's a process that works for me."

"So, how I can help?"

"Why don't you tell me about your husband."

She looked queasy. "Like, what?"

"What kind of music did he listen to?"

"He liked pop rock. It was kind of funny because he was this super-erudite professor. I mean, he wore a bowtie to class and everything. But over the summer, he insisted we go to the Taylor Swift concert. It was me, him, and fifty thousand teenaged girls. He *loved* it." She covered her mouth and laughed.

Bodhi smiled at her. "Did he play any sports?"

"He played tennis sometimes. He liked to swim, too. He'd get up early most mornings and swim laps at the JCC pool before work."

"Did he do that the day he died?"

She thought for a moment. "He did. He got up before I did and went to the pool. He stopped and picked up bagels and cream cheese on his way home. We had breakfast together before he headed to campus."

"Do you work?"

She shook her head. "I got my undergraduate degree in history. A month later we got married. I'd always planned to go for my master's and then a Ph.D., but ... it got weird. Giles was the head of the department and nobody wanted to be my advisor because it would put them in an awkward spot. I just ... I stopped taking classes. I always figured I'd go back. But it's been three and a half years since I left the program. Now, I don't know anymore."

He gently brought her back to the day her husband died. "So, after breakfast, Giles went to work. Do you remember what you did?"

"I went to the grocery store. We had that big snowfall over the weekend, and Giant Eagle had completely sold out of milk. I'd tried to pick some up on Monday, and the truck hadn't come in yet. The guy stocking the dairy shelves told me they'd be getting a delivery on Tuesday morning, so right after Giles left, I went to the store."

"Did you get milk?"

"I sure did. As well as bread and toilet paper." She giggled.

"Ah, the holy trinity. You'll be ready for the next storm."

Her smile faded. "Then I returned some library books and picked up the dry cleaning. All the stereotypical homemaker duties."

"What time did Giles come home?"

"He was home by three. He doesn't—didn't—have Tuesday office hours. We went to the hardware store to look at bathroom fixtures. We were planning to remodel the master bath. After that, he made himself some pasta and a salad for dinner. I kept him company while he ate, even though I don't eat myself until after yoga. Then I left for my yoga class. And when I came back ...." She tipped her head back against the mantle and closed her eyes.

He watched her for a moment. Then he turned away to give her some privacy. As he scanned the bookshelves closest to the window, the back of his neck began to tingle. He turned to look through the big bay window behind the sofa. Across the street, Hope's neighbor stood at her own big bay window, pulling a sheer curtain to the side, and stared directly into the Hope's family room.

Creepy. Or urgent.

Hope's voice interrupted his thoughts. "Dr. King?"

"Yes?"

"I just needed a second. I'm sorry about that."

"Please, don't apologize."

She swayed on her feet. He gave her a closer look. Her skin looked almost translucent.

"Have you been eating?"

She nodded but didn't meet his eyes.

"Why don't you sit down. I'll get you some tea and toast. Or juice and crackers. Something."

She collapsed into the chair and waved vaguely toward the back of the house. "I don't know what's out there. There's a bunch of casseroles in the freezer. I keep forgetting to defrost them."

He placed a hand on her shoulder. "Don't worry. I'll find something."

He walked through the connected formal dining room, which was still and dark—a room that saw little use—and into the bright kitchen. A kettle sat waiting on the stovetop. He filled it with water from the sink's faucet and set it to boil while he assessed the contents of the pantry. A tea tin, a box of soup crackers, half a loaf of bread, some onions, and dried pasta.

As he reached for the bread, he knocked over a stack of cookbooks that were piled haphazardly on the wire shelf. He bent to gather them into a pile and noticed a soft leather-bound volume stuck in between a glossy *Joy of Cooking* that looked as if it had never been opened and a well-thumbed copy of *One-Pot Meals for Two*. He picked up the thick book and turned it over. It was a copy of the King James Version of the Bible with the words *Family Bible* embossed on the cover and the spine in gold letters.

He wrinkled his brow. The Bible had clearly gotten mixed in with the cookbooks by accident. It was out of place in the pantry. It belonged on the shelf in the family room, right next to the Chumash. He placed it on the counter where Hope would see it and stacked the recipe books on the pantry shelf.

Then he dropped a slice of bread into the toaster and pressed the lever. While the bread toasted, he scared up an apple, which he washed and sliced. He dug a lasagna from the tower of casserole dishes in the overstuffed freezer and placed it on the counter to thaw.

The kettle whistled. He steeped a teabag, buttered the toast, took down a jar of honey from the cabinet near the mugs, and put the meager offerings on a tray he found leaning against the backsplash behind the sink.

When he returned to the living room, Hope looked livelier. Or at least less on the verge of fainting. He placed the tray on the side table next to her chair.

"Thank you, Dr. King. I'm embarrassed to say I haven't been taking the best care of myself." She kept her eyes downcast, hidden by her eyelashes.

"Do you want me to call a social worker? Someone who can check on you, maybe keep you company for a few days?"

"No, I'm fine. Honestly. Mrs. Remmy across the street checks on me all the time. And my friends call and stop by when they can." She lifted the teacup with a shaky hand and sipped the hot drink.

"Even so, you seem ..." He'd been about to say 'frail'

or 'delicate,' but both words carried a whiff of sexist condescension, so he trailed off.

"I know I need to be better about my sleep and nutrition." She lifted her eyes to his. "I battled leukemia a few years ago. It's in remission, but I know all about fatigue and rest. Trust me."

"If you're sure—"

"I'm positive. But, would it be okay if we finished this discussion some other time? I know you need to know about Giles, but I ... can't right now." Her voice shook and tears leaked out her eyes.

"Absolutely." He reached into his pocket for the handkerchief he'd gotten into the habit of carrying when he lived in Burma, where paper products could be hard to come by.

"I do want to help you," she whispered.

"I know." He crouched by her chair and wiped the tears from her eyes with the corner of the handkerchief. "Eat that. I put a lasagna on your counter to defrost. You should warm that up later."

She nibbled the toast. "I'll move it to the fridge and eat it tomorrow."

He held her gaze but said nothing.

"I will," she insisted.

"Good. I'll let myself out."

She made a noise of protest but he gave her a stern look. "Don't you dare get up."

She sank back against the chair. "You've been so kind to me. Thank you."

He looked down at her drawn, sad face for a long moment. "You're welcome. After you've eaten, don't forget to lock the door behind me."

"I won't," she promised.

He walked to the door. As he twisted the knob and pushed it open, he spotted the curtain in Mrs. Remmy's living room swinging. He watched her door and window as he put on his helmet and slowly wheeled his bike down the steps, but he didn't see the neighbor woman again.

CHAPTER EIGHTEEN

"Standing over my shoulder and growling doesn't make the computer work faster. You know that, right?" Chrys didn't turn to look at him as she said the words.

Burton ignored her grumbling and watched her fingers fly over the keyboard, typing in combinations of names, addresses, dates, and Social Security numbers.

"Lewis must be confused," Chrys continued for the umpteenth time, still staring at the monitor. "Tenley doesn't have a sister. He's an only child."

A thought buzzed in Burton's ear, like a bee. Or like Chrys' barely restrained irritation.

He snapped his fingers. "Hang on. Lewis also said Tenley's parents died of cancer, but they died in a car crash when he was just a kid."

This time, she craned her neck to meet his eyes. "You think Tenley invented a personal history for his Army buddies? Could be, if he leans toward the sociopathic."

"That's a possibility, but no. I'm thinking Tenley was raised by this distant cousin of his mom's from the time he was, what, four? He probably considered her and her husband to be his parents, even if they never formally adopted him."

"And that would make *their* kid his sister in his mind. You might be on to something, old man." Her eyes sparked with excitement, and her fingers moved even faster, blurring as she typed furiously.

Old man? What the ... no time for it now. He'd have to lick his wounds later.

"Did the people who raised Tenley have kids of their own?"

"Hold your horses, I'm looking."

He clamped his mouth closed and waited, listening to the clicking of the keys and the faint whine of the desktop computer's fan. After a minute, she used the mouse to pull up a file and hit print.

He walked over to the printer in the corner of the room and caught the page as it emerged.

"Hot off the presses."

She joined him and pointed to a line about a third of

the way down the page. "The Kesslers had one biological child. A girl, five years younger than Damon Tenley. So she would have been born about a year after Tenley came to live with them."

"They might be close. Big brother and baby sister." He slapped his thigh. "Let's go talk to her."

"Minor problem. The girl, Anastasia H. Kessler, dropped off the map in late 2011, after her mother died."

"You're kidding."

Her right eyebrow shot up to her hairline, and she pinned him with a sour look. "Yeah, Burton. This is my idea of a joke. Isn't it hilarious?"

He leveled her with a look of his own. "What's her last known address?"

"The house in Stanton Heights."

"Where Tenley stayed when he came back to town?"

"Yeah. She cleared out in 2011 and left no forwarding address. That squares with Tenley asking Van Lewis to bring in his mail. He was living there alone. The house was on the market for all of 2012 and 2013."

"Did it sell?"

She shook her head. "No record of a transfer. But Lewis had that part right. The house is in his name, not hers."

"They left the house to Tenley, not their own daughter?"

"I'm sure they considered him a son, Burton. And he's five years older. So when the mother died, Anastasia would've been twenty or twenty-one, give or take. That's a lot of responsibility to dump on a college-aged kid."

"I guess. Pretty curious this *kid* disappeared without a trace. You're sure Anastasia Kessler wasn't on Tenley's visitors list at the prison?"

"My guy said Van Lewis was his only visitor."

Burton was about to suggest paying a visit to Tenley's house when his cell phone rang in his pocket.

He pulled it out and barked, "Gilbert."

"Detective Gilbert, it's Bodhi King."

The pathologist sounded winded.

"Everything okay, Dr. King? It sounds like you're out of breath."

"Just pushing my bike along while we talk. I'm not coordinated enough to talk and ride."

"Sure. What can I do for you?"

"I was talking to Hope Noor at her home."

"Yeah? Did she have any ideas about how Tenley's DNA got there?"

"Not that she shared. I'm calling to ask whether anyone's interviewed the neighbor who lives across the street?"

"Mrs. Remmy? Yeah. Uniforms canvassed the entire block. Why? What about her?"

"Mrs. Noor mentioned an argument she and her husband had the night he died—"

"A fight?" Burton's blood pressure surged. Vitanni's notes from the interview with Hope Noor didn't reference a fight.

"A fight sounds like it might be physical. My takeaway from Mrs. Noor was this was a verbal altercation. And I have a suspicion the neighbor may have overheard some or all of it."

Burton gritted his teeth. After thirty-four years on the force, he knew he shouldn't be surprised to learn that even the most law-abiding citizens seemed to have selective recall when it came to telling law enforcement what they knew. But it burned him up every time.

Odds were, the argument was innocuous and unrelated to Giles Noor's murder. Odds were, Hope Noor was embarrassed to mention it, and the neighbor didn't want to come across as a busybody. But there was a reason Burton never played the lottery: a homicide detective knows better than to trust the odds.

He sighed. "Thanks for passing it along. We'll send a unit out to reinterview the neighbor."

"Great. Will you do it soon? She kept watching me

from her window. I think she's in the mood to talk. Might as well strike while the iron's hot."

"We'll get someone out there as soon as we can. Right now our priority is finding Anastasia Kessler."

"Who?"

Why did he open his big trap?

"Anastasia Kessler. The family who took Tenley in after his parents died were named Kessler. They apparently had a daughter five years younger than Tenley. One of Tenley's Army buddies mentioned a sister he was close with, so we need to run her down. Any other questions?"

Chrys' eyes widened at his snotty tone. He shrugged at her. Did she see him calling Bodhi King up and telling him how to remove eyeballs from corpses or how to weigh livers?

"No. Sorry to have bothered you, detective."

"No problem." He ended the call and pocketed the phone.

CHAPTER NINETEEN

That neighbor of Hope's knows something. The thought circled around Bodhi's brain to the rhythm of his pedaling. But Detectives Burton and Martin hadn't taken him seriously.

He tried to shrug it off as he coasted down the hill to Shadyside's business district. He'd passed along the information. That was all he could do.

He stopped in front of the combination tea shop/bookstore that was, conveniently enough, located around the corner from Maisy's loft apartment. He checked his watch. He had a half an hour before he needed to meet Maisy. Definitely enough time for a cup of oolong tea and a spin through the used mystery section.

He locked his bike to the rack at the edge of the parking lot next to the building and jogged down the stairs to the shop's entrance, one story below street level. He opened the door, stepped inside, and inhaled the heady perfume of old books and fragrant teas. Warm air drove away the chill outside, and the shop hummed with low voices as people browsed the shelves or sat at over-stuffed couches or small tables and nibbled on treats from the cafe while they sipped tisanes, teas, and hot chocolate.

He had it on good authority that nobody drank the coffee as it was "slightly stronger than brown water." But everything else on the menu ranged from serviceable to great.

He ordered a mug of tea and a sesame cookie and thumbed through the stack of graphic novels by the register while he waited for his order.

"As I live and breathe, is that Bodhi King?" a syrupy voice gasped behind him as he juggled his tea and treat through the short line at the counter.

That Southern fried voice could belong to only one person. He pivoted and nearly spilled scalding hot tea down the front of Pittsburgh's most-beloved weather girl turned investigative reporter as she flung her arms around his torso and squeezed.

"Maisy, what are you doing here?" he wheezed.

She released him and pointed to the cushioned window bench. "I'm meetin' a source, sugar. What are *you* doing here?"

"My interview ended early, so I thought I'd hang out here until it was time for us to meet."

"Too funny. Well, come on, you can meet Penny." She hooked her arm through his and started to tug him toward the built-in window seat.

"Aren't you working?"

"She's sort of a dud," Maisy whispered near his ear. "She's a lawyer, and, just like a lawyer, she qualifies *everything* she says with 'ifs, purportedlys, and for the sake of arguments.' Talk about a snoozer of an exposé." She faked a dramatic, wide yawn.

He laughed despite himself. "What are you exposing?"

"You, as a matter of fact."

"Pardon?"

"Well, not *you*. The M.E.'s office. And the D.A.'s office. I know, I know, you're thinking, now Maisy, how could a story *that* juicy be a dud? Well, I'm here to tell you, Penelope Geoffries manages to suck the excitement right out of it. Like that." She snapped her fingers.

"Geoffries? With the public defender's office?"

"Oh, you know her?"

"No, but Maisy. I don't think this is a good—"

Maisy came to a sudden stop in front of a freckled woman who wore her hair in a sensible bob. She gave Bodhi a warm smile that lit up her face.

"Penny, you'll never believe it, but this here is Bodhi King."

"Ms. Geoffries, it's nice to meet you." Bodhi returned the smile and gestured with his tea and his cookie in lieu of offering his hand.

"You, as well." She flashed Maisy a confused look.

"Bodhi's the consultant I told you about—the smart cookie the medical examiner called in to figure out how your client's DNA results went catawampus."

Penny blinked. "I ... I don't think we should be talking about Damon. No offense, Dr. King."

"You're talking to me, sugar," Maisy pointed out to the public defender.

Penny gave her a stiff smile. "That's different. We're discussing the conditions under which Mr. Tenley would consider sitting down with you for an interview. Dr. King is working against Damon's interests."

"I completely understand. I didn't mean to intrude on your conversation. Maisy, I'll talk to you later, the way we'd planned. I really just want to eat my cookie and find some good books." He started to back away.

"Wait. Penny, at least tell him what you were just saying to me. That's not any sort of confidential or privileged client information, is it?" Maisy turned her baby blues on the lawyer and gave her a pleading expression.

The way the legal terms rolled off Maisy's tongue gave the lie to her ditzy confusion about legal ethics. Bodhi suppressed a smile. From the look on Penny's face, she wasn't fooled either. But she did nod.

"I'm not going to waste your time or mine trying to convince you my client's a person. But he is. And, as a citizen of the United States, he has a Constitutional right to any evidence that may prove exculpatory—a fact the district attorney seems to have forgotten." The color rose in her cheeks, and her eyes blazed.

"Ms. Geoffries, I'm not a lawyer. I don't know the legal standard that governs here. My role, my *only* role, is to determine how your client's DNA could possibly have been found at Giles Noor's murder scene. And I promise you, if I learn that there was any problem with the original DNA testing, I'll take it straight to District Attorney Ford. And if she doesn't turn it over to you, I'll bring it to you myself."

Penny Geoffries rolled her eyes skyward.

"No, no, don't go rolling your eyes. Bodhi's a straight shooter. He's a Buddhist. It's against his religion to lie, isn't that right, hon?"

"Not ... exactly. It's true that the fourth precept is to refrain from incorrect speech. But the precepts aren't like the Ten Commandments or anything."

"See?" Maisy said triumphantly, as if he'd proved her point.

Penny laughed grudgingly. "Well, it's good to know there's someone like you on the other side."

"But, Bodhi, Damon Tenley really doesn't sound irredeemable. Tell him, Penny."

He considered telling Maisy the Buddha teaches that no living being is irredeemable, but the prospect of how she might misinterpret that teaching stopped him.

"Tell him what, about Damon's sister?"

"Yes," Maisy confirmed.

"I thought Mr. Tenley was an only child?" Bodhi was careful not to show too much interest in the subject.

"Yes, biologically, he was. But Frank and Lisa Kessler, the distant relatives who took him in after his mother and father died, raised him from the age of four. Even though they never formally adopted him or changed his name, they were Damon Tenley's parents. And when they had a baby girl just after he turned five, she was his sister." Passion flared in the public defender's voice.

He remembered the nickname Meghan used in

talking about her. 'Passionate Penny.' He could see where it had come from.

"They were close?"

Maisy broke in, "Close? Sugar, he saved her life!"

Bodhi turned to the lawyer. "Did he really?"

"He really did. Frank Kessler died in 2010. Lisa died a year later in 2011. By the time Lisa was in hospice care, the daughter—Anastasia—learned she had leukemia. She delayed treatment to care for her mom. Damon, of course, was serving in the army during this time. When he separated from the military in October 2012, Anastasia was very, very sick. The oncologists recommended a bone marrow transplant."

"Damon was a match?"

"Right. He jumped at the chance to help his younger sister. A few weeks after he returned home, they underwent the harvesting and transplant procedures." Penny's chest heaved as she recounted the story. "He only told me about it because he was in the county jail when the time came for Anastasia's second follow-up appointment, and he was so worried she'd have to go alone. He wanted me to go with her."

His curiosity got the better of him. "Did you?"

"I can't get involved in my clients' personal lives like that, Dr. King."

He waited.

"But I did call a friend of mine who's a social worker. She called Ms. Kessler and offered to accompany her. Ms. Kessler declined."

"Did Anastasia visit Damon in jail?"

Penny sighed. "No. She didn't visit him and she didn't attend his trial. I'd hoped to call her at trial as a character witness, but the number Damon had for her was disconnected when I tried to reach her. I had my investigator try to track her down, but frankly, we were gearing up for the trial and had bigger fish to fry. The point of the story, Dr. King, is that Damon Tenley, like most people, is complex and contradictory. He's not just a monster."

That may have been the point the attorney intended to make. But Bodhi had a different takeaway. Something she said was rattling around in his brain. There was a connection, an important one, that he needed time, space, and quiet to focus on.

"Thanks for talking to me, Ms. Geoffries."

"Of course."

He inclined his head toward Maisy. "Maisy, I'm going to have to reschedule our chat. I'm sorry."

She proffered her cheek for a kiss, which he delivered. "I'm gonna hold you to that, Bodhi."

"Please do."

He drank the last sip of his tea and dropped the mug in the bin near the door. Then he sprinted up the stairs and fumbled with the lock on his bike as he called Saul to cancel their dinner, too.

CHAPTER TWENTY

H ope sat in the chair for a long time after Bodhi King left. She stared absently at the framed photographs hanging on the opposite wall, a collection of memories from trips she and Giles had taken. She ate the buttered toast without tasting it and drank the tea.

The forensic pathologist wasn't at all what she'd expected. She'd imagined him as a loud, confident guy with slicked-back hair and bright white teeth who wore a sharp suit and made bold declarations. Instead, she got a soft-spoken, curly-haired man who asked gentle questions and fed her tea and toast. He'd been a comforting presence, for sure, and her home felt empty with him gone. But there was no way *that* guy—he rode a bicycle, for Pete's sake—was going to figure out how Damon

Tenley's DNA managed to turn up at the scene of her husband's murder. *Not a chance.*

Finally, long after the weak winter sun had sunk behind a gray horizon, she pushed herself to her feet. She pressed the switch beside the mantle to turn off the fire. Either emotion or exhaustion got the better of her for a moment, and she stumbled.

She threw out a hand and caught the edge of the bookshelf. When she was sure she was steady on her feet, she picked up the tray and carried it out to the kitchen. As she placed the dirty dishes in the sink, her eyes fell on the family Bible sitting on the counter and her heart thumped against her rib cage.

How did that get there?

She never should've kept it. She'd tucked it away for years, nestled in the bottom of trunk under a small stack of quilts and blankets her mother had made and some photo albums from her childhood. Family heirlooms—if one used the term *heirloom* loosely—that she couldn't bring herself to leave behind when she started her life with Giles but that she hadn't wanted to see as a daily reminder of her old life.

She'd been looking for the warm crocheted bedspread her mother had worked on while she was undergoing her final chemotherapy treatments. Mom had used three different shades of blue in the pattern, and Hope thought it would look gorgeous in the bedroom, especially after she and Giles finished remodeling the en suite bath in the colors of the ocean.

Giles had found her kneeling by the trunk in the basement, clutching the afghan to her chest. He helped her to her feet, wiped away her tears, and pulled her against his chest in a tight embrace. Then he'd noticed the Bible cradled in the bottom of the trunk.

Ever the historian, his eyes had lit with interest, and he asked if he could remove it from the trunk.

She was trapped.

So she'd nodded reluctantly, and he'd lifted the book gingerly from the trunk with all the eagerness one might expect from a historian. He'd run his hands over the cover with something approaching awe and had announced that it deserved a place of honor on their bookshelves. She willed him not to flip the pages open.

"No," she'd snapped. "I don't want to see it everyday. It's ... too painful." She'd stuffed it back into the trunk and turned the key in the lock.

He'd gathered her into his arms and whispered soothing words about her dead parents, more concerned about her emotional state than the musty old book. But she'd spent weeks on edge, worried that he'd grow curious about it, go looking for the key, and flip through the pages. Every time she walked through the basement, she was hyper-aware of the Bible. She could feel its presence as it sat in the trunk, an unexploded land mine, waiting to blow her to pieces.

But, Giles hadn't shown any interest in it, and after a while, her anxiety had faded. Giles hadn't been particularly religious, and despite its age, the Christian Bible probably hadn't held much appeal for him. She forgot all about the thing.

Then, last week, after she'd relaxed, it happened.

She'd traipsed down the stairs in her yoga pants with her mat tucked under her arm and called his name to say goodbye before she left for class.

"Hope?" he answered in a strangled voice. "I'm in here."

She headed into the family room and froze in the doorway. He was sitting beside the fire, a glass of wine in one hand and the Family Bible in the other.

Her heart thrummed and her chest constricted.

They locked eyes for what felt like a decade. Hope's frantic pulse made it hard to think, let alone speak, but she managed to squeak out some words. "I've got to run. I'm picking Zoe up for class."

"Hope. We need to talk about this." He gestured with the Bible.

"Sure. When I get home." She turned up the corners of her mouth in what she hoped was a smile.

"No, we need to talk now." He placed his wineglass on the side table with exaggerated care and flipped open the book to the family records pages.

And she'd lost it. One minute, her mind was scrabbling like an animal trying to find purchase on shifting ground. The next, she was screaming at Giles, a jumble of accusations and excuses. He sat, motionless and silent, and stared at her. She didn't know how long she'd railed—a long time, for sure. When her throat was raw, she sagged against the wall, limp and exhausted, until she stopped shaking.

Then she took her purple winter jacket from the coat closet in the hall and put it on. Her movements seemed jerky and unnatural to her. She zippered the jacket up to her chin and jammed a hat down over her ponytail.

"I'm going to class. We can talk more when I get home."

He nodded stiffly, his eyes never leaving her face as she walked toward the door.

But when she returned later that night, Giles was already in bed.

Hope shuddered at the memory and pulled her hand away from the Bible. She should have gotten rid of it for sure before she'd called the police. But, she'd panicked and tossed it in with the cookbooks. Now, here it was again. Her past threatening her future. She could only hope Bodhi King hadn't opened it.

She knew what she needed to do. She just had to have the will to do it.

But first, she needed a solid night's sleep. She shook out two sedatives from her prescription bottle. Then she poured herself a generous glass of wine and ascended the back staircase to spend one last night in the home she'd shared with Giles.

CHAPTER TWENTY-ONE

By the time Bodhi biked home, the sun had set, and he was chilled through by the cold night air. He stowed his bicycle in the front hallway, turned on some lights, greeted Eliza Doolittle, and reheated a serving of the vegetarian chili he'd made earlier in the week.

After he ate his fill of the hot, hearty chili, he cleaned up the kitchen then sat for a short, but necessary, meditation. It seemed indulgent to spend time sitting now, when time seemed to be very much of the essence. But long experience had taught him that hurrying was always a waste of precious time. Better to center his mind and energy so as to spend the hours ahead as productively as possible.

So he sat, closed his eyes, and focused on his breath.

Hope Noor's pale, tortured face pushed its way into his mind's eye, over and over. Over and over, he gently closed the door on the image and returned to his breath.

The clock in the living room ticked softly. The macaw sang to herself. The cold seeped from the floorboards through his socks to his toes. And he sat.

When he felt ready, he opened his eyes and allowed his surrounds to return to the foreground. It had been a long while since he'd had such a distracted meditation session. But thoughts of the widow had persistently intruded on him. Hope had an almost childlike quality about her—it stirred an instinct to protect her.

Which made what he was about to do seem even more ethically questionable than it was. But he didn't see another way.

He rummaged through his backpack until he found his address book. As he flipped through it, looking for the contact who could help him, he remembered Bette's exaggerated amazement at learning that he kept a paper address book, and he smiled at the memory.

"Found it, Eliza Doolittle," he informed the bird, marking an entry with his finger while he pulled his phone from his pocket.

"Good for Bodhi. Good boy," the macaw praised him. "Treat? Treat."

He checked the time. It was not quite five-thirty.

There was a better than even chance of reaching Jim at his desk. He punched in the number. While he waited for the call to connect, he shook out a handful of dried cranberries for the bird and held out his palm. "I'm the good boy, but you get the treat. How's that work?"

"Smart bird," she cawed.

He tended to agree.

"Cumberland County Criminal Investigations. Jim Shore speaking."

"Jim, hi. It's Bodhi King. We met the year before last in Québec City at the North American Society of Forensic Pathology conference."

"Sure, sure, I remember. You were on the black swans panel. Your stories were some humdingers." He chuckled.

"Yeah, I guess they were. And I remember you mentioned your district attorney's office had just gotten one of those new rapid DNA testing machines, right?"

"That's right! We only started using it the week before the meeting, and you know what? Right after I got back from Canada, we caught our first murderer with it."

"Really?"

"True story. So what can I do for you?"

Bodhi figured he might as well come right out with it. Shading the request or hinting at what he needed was disrespectful of Jim and his time.

"I need a big favor. If I drive out there tonight, will you let me use your machine?"

Jim made a *humph* noise, a cross between *let me see* and *I don't think so*. Bodhi waited.

"The thing is, the cartridges are pricey. We get a discount for buying in bulk, but even so, each one works out to about a hundred dollars. I'd be happy to run a sample for you ... but I'm afraid you'd have to pony up for the cartridge. They're single use, so it's sort of a big deal."

"That's no problem at all," Bodhi assured him.

"In that case, sure, I'd be happy to. How soon can you get here?"

"Well, I'm in Pittsburgh, so it'll take me three hours to get to Carlisle if everything goes well. Say between eight-thirty and nine?"

"That's fine. I'm a bit of a night owl. I'll go home, grab a bite with the missus and plan on being back here no later than eight-thirty. But, surely, the Allegheny County crime lab's got fancier machines that we do. They're world class." He laughed.

"I agree, it's a great lab. In fact, I need to test this sample for a matter the Allegheny County medical examiner has asked me to consult on. But, for reasons I can't go into right now, it's crucial that I use a different lab. And, as far as I know, they don't have a rapid DNA machine."

"I knew we were one of the first in the state to get one, but I sort of assumed Pittsburgh and Philly got them soon after."

"As far as I know, Philadelphia's medical examiner's office doesn't have one either, although some local police departments out that way may."

Bodhi knew from talking with Saul that the speed of rapid DNA testing was its sizable advantage, but that many pathologists and serologists alike agreed the downsides were legion and included such doozies as reliability, reproducibility, and sensitivity. But there was no reason to get into any of those issues with Jim. For Bodhi's present purposes, a rapid DNA test would be more than adequate.

"Well, how about that? Anyway, sure, I'll help you out."

"Thanks, Jim. You're a real lifesaver. I can't tell you how much I appreciate this."

"You bet; happy to help out. Is this your cell phone you're calling from?"

"It is."

"Tell you what—I'll send you a text from my phone, so you'll have my number. That way, you can give me a call or text me back when you get off the Turnpike and

I'll get in here, turn on the lights, and warm up the computers and the equipment."

"That sounds like a great plan."

"Drive safe. I'll see you in a bit."

Jim ended the call. Bodhi tossed an extra notebook and a phone charger into his backpack, filled his water bottle, and refilled Eliza Doolittle's food and water bowls.

"You're in charge until I get back."

"Eliza's in charge always," the bird corrected him.

He shook his head and dug his tenant's car keys out of her kitchen junk drawer. She'd told him time and again that he was welcome to drive her little VW bug whenever he liked, but aside from taking the bird to the vet, he'd been able to bike everywhere he needed to go. He grabbed a packet of post-it notes and a pencil so he'd remember to mark his mileage and reimburse her for the wear and tear on her vehicle. Then he put on his coat, patted his pocket to make sure he had everything, and turned out the kitchen lights, leaving the light over the stove on for the macaw.

CHAPTER TWENTY-TWO

Chrys twisted the key in the ignition, killing the engine. Burton sat in the passenger seat and eyed the dark, deserted house.

"Are we getting out or what?" she asked.

He puffed out his cheeks and exhaled, craning his neck from left to right. "I guess. For all the good it'll do. Look at this street. It's dead."

The house Tenley had inherited sat at the bend of a curving street cut into one of Stanton Heights' steep hillsides. The neighborhood was a seemingly random mix of ranch-style homes, traditional brick two stories, old rowhouses, and newer custom built homes. The assorted structures housed an equally eclectic collection of occupants. There were teachers, as well as municipal employees, firefighters, and police officers who were obligated to live within the city limits—although the Fraternal Order of Police had recently spent Burton's dues arguing the issue all the way to the Supreme Court and, apparently, had won the right for the law enforcement officers to move out to ritzy suburbs they couldn't afford anyway. In addition, there was the usual mix of senior citizens, empty nesters, and young parents. And, no doubt, an increasing number of gentrifiers who'd been lured to town by the influx of technology companies and who were gradually pricing the neighborhood out of the reach of its original residents.

Given the aging sedans parked in the driveways and the naked awning frames fronting the faded but well-kept homes, this street skewed toward the older end of the neighborhood demographic. He pictured tightly rolled, striped fabric awnings, standing sentinel in every shed and garage, waiting for the spring thaw, when they'd be unfurled and replaced, just before the porches were broom-swept or vacuumed (depending on the absence or presence of outdoor carpeting).

Chrys nodded in agreement. "I thought we'd catch some office workers coming home from work, but I don't see a soul."

"This crowd is probably mainly retirees. If we start banging on doors now, in the dark, we're begging for someone to slap us with a complaint."

"So what do you want to do?"

"We're here. We might as well take a quick walk around the perimeter of Tenley's place. If we catch the attention of a nosy neighbor then, bonus, we get to have a conversation without banging on any doors."

She twisted her lips. "You do remember what color our skin is and the minor fact that we aren't in uniform, right? I'd rather be hit by a complaint than a bullet."

"You worry too much, Martin. This is a quiet neighborhood." All the same, he checked his weapon before they exited the vehicle.

She gave him a dark look and mirrored his actions, muttering under her breath. They stepped over a pile of dirty slush and stood shoulder to shoulder on the sidewalk, looking up at the yellow house where Damon Tenley and Anastasia Kessler had grown up. A pair of green velvet curtains covered the picture window to the left of the frosted glass door.

"I guess we ought to at least ring the bell first—in case someone's squatting in there or a couple of teens are using the place as a love nest."

"Gross," Chrys said.

He didn't disagree. But he wouldn't be surprised to find someone inside.

"Come on."

He mounted the green-carpeted steps a few feet

ahead of Chrys and waited for her on the porch. He rested his right hand on the butt of his weapon. When she joined him, he stretched forward and leaned on the doorbell for a long moment before resuming his ready position.

She tilted an ear toward the door and squinted as if that would help her hear better. "I didn't hear a chime. Did you?"

"Nah. Figures. The power's probably been turned off for years."

He raised his fist and hammered on the door. The pounding resounded along the silent street. He and Chrys swept their heads in unison from left to right, looking for alarmed neighbors who might be peeking out from behind their curtains but saw no movement.

"Knock again," she said.

He did. Louder this time.

"Well if anyone is in there, they've had ample warning." He sidestepped to his right and flipped open the black metal mailbox mounted to the yellow brick facade.

"You're gonna disturb a nest of spiders," she warned him.

"Do spiders even nest?"

She shrugged. He grinned at her and dug his black leather gloves out of his coat pockets. After snapping them on, he plunged his hand into the depth of the box and emerged with a fistful of junk mail and zero spiders. He handed her half the stack. She pulled out her cellphone and activated the flashlight app. He moved a step closer, put his stack of mail inside the arc of light, and began to flip through the envelopes and advertising circulars.

Resident, Resident, Frank Kessler or Current Resident, Current Resident, Lisa Kessler, Safe Driver, Resident, A. H. Kessler, Anastasia Kessler .... The rest were all addressed to Resident.

"Nothing here. One ad for frozen yogurt addressed to Anastasia and one credit card offer for A. H. Kessler, presumably that's her, too. What've you got?"

"A whole lot of nothing. Mostly 'resident' crap. An offer addressed to Damon to save money and energy by installing solar panels—"

"He's saving even more as a permanent guest of the commonwealth." Burton chuckled at his own joke.

She went on as if he hadn't interrupted, "Some catalogues addressed to Anastasia .... And a schedule from one of those fancy exercise studios with the barre classes. It's addressed to someone named Olivia Scott."

"Yes!" He pumped his gloved fist.

"Can we celebrate in the car? I'm freezing my butt off out here." She thumbed off the flashlight app.

He blinked hard several times in an effort to help his

eyes adjust to the dark. He was about to suggest they at least check out the backyard first, but when he refocused his eyes, Chrys was already on her way down the stairs.

A bright white LED light clicked on at the house to the right of Tenley's place. The door swung open, and a woman peered out at him. "Excuse me," she called.

At the sound of her voice, Chrys turned around and trotted back up the stairs.

"Yes, ma'am?" Burton said.

"Did our knocking disturb you, ma'am?" Chrys asked.

The woman frowned and shook her head. She eyed their pantsuits and long wool coats. "No. Are you folks realtors?" she asked in a hopeful voice.

"Ah, sorry, no. We're detectives. I'm Burton Gilbert, and this is my partner, Chrys Martin." He flashed his badge. Beside him Chrys did the same.

The woman stepped out onto her porch. Then she came to the edge and hung over the railing to peer at their identification.

"You here about Damon?" She shook her head in sorrow. "He was a good boy growing up. A polite young man. I can't imagine what happened to him."

"Actually, Mrs...." Chrys trailed off to let the woman supply her name.

"Angela Antolini."

"Mrs. Antolini, we're interested in speaking to Anastasia Kessler. Do you know where we can find her?"

"It's cold out here. Channel Eleven says we're gonna get snow overnight. Why don't you two come inside?"

They exchanged glances.

"That's very kind of you, Mrs. Antolini." Burton gave her his friendliest smile, and they tromped down to the sidewalk and hurried up her steps before she could change her mind.

CHAPTER TWENTY-THREE

Bodhi slowed the car to drive through the tollbooth lane, activating the E-ZPass reader, as he entered the turnpike at the Allegheny Valley Interchange and pointed the car east toward Harrisburg. He'd have to remember to add the turnpike fees to his sticky note of expenses.

After he cleared the booth and merged onto the highway, he used his phone's voice command feature to call Saul at home. He was careful to keep his eyes on the dark road stretched out in front of him.

As a rule, he was a monotasker. He'd read the studies that showed multitasking caused what the experts called *attention residue*, which occurred when part of the brain was still distracted by thoughts of the previous task even after a person had moved on to the next. But more than that, he'd spent most of his adult life practicing mindfulness, focusing on being present and devoting his attention to the moment. Sometimes, though, circumstances demanded he split his attention.

Saul's wife, Mona, answered the phone. "David residence."

Her lilting voice gave no hint to any chaos that might be happening in the background. But Bodhi suspected that, with four kids, the David residence was sure to be chaotic during the post-school/work hours of a weeknight.

"Hi, Mona. It's Bodhi. Could I speak to Saul?"

"Bodhi! Have you changed your mind about dinner? We're just about to sit down. I can keep it warm until you get here."

"That's a gracious offer, and I really am very sorry for backing out on short notice, but a work emergency came up. I'm actually headed out of town for the night. I hope we can do it sometime next week?"

She laughed. "You know, we *do* eat dinner every night. There's no need to be formal about it. Just show up at dinner time and we'll fix you a plate. You're welcome any time."

"Thanks, Mona."

"No thanks needed, we'd love to have you. Now let me get Saul for you."

He heard her tell one of the boys to let their father know he had a phone call. A moment later, Saul's voice boomed through his phone's speaker.

"What's up, Bodhi?"

"I'm following up a hunch. I'm not necessarily following your office's standard operating procedures—"

"Color me shocked," Saul interjected in a dry voice.

"—so the fewer details you know, the better. I need Tory Thurmont's home number, if you have it handy."

"It's only six-thirty. You can probably still catch her at the lab."

"I know. I don't want to talk to her now. But I am going to need to talk to her later. I didn't want to risk waking up your kids."

"Why can't you call her now and get her home number?"

Bodhi exhaled. "Because she'll want to know what I'm doing; and if I tell her, she'll probably try to stop me. I want to wait to speak to her until the die's been cast and it's too late to do anything about it."

"What?"

"You asked."

Saul was silent for a long moment.

"And you hired me," Bodhi pointed out. "You know how I operate."

Saul grumbled something unintelligible.

"So can you maybe text the number to me from your cell phone? I'm about to go through a tunnel and I might lose you."

"Which tunnel? Fort Pitt? Squirrel Hill? Liberty? Bodhi, where *are* you?"

"Uh, no, the Tuscarora Mountain Tunnel." He smiled to himself.

It was technically true. He *was* about to go through the tunnel. In another hour or so. It was, as his monk friends would say, a true lie. It reminded him of the story of the time the Buddha saw a man sprinting through the forest as if being chased. The Buddha moved several feet away from his original spot. Seconds later a band of robbers came along. They turned to the Buddha and demanded if he'd seen a man run by while he'd been standing there. The Buddha answered, truthfully, 'no.' After all, he hadn't been standing in *that* spot when the man had run by.

"On the turnpike?" Saul demanded.

"Is there another one?"

"What are you up to? No, never mind, you're right. Don't tell me. I'll send you her number. Listen, you be careful. Apparently there's a winter storm headed our way."

"Thanks, Saul. See you tomorrow."

He ended the call and peered through the windshield. The lights from the tractor trailers speeding by on his left smeared into blurred trails in the darkness as the little car rocked from side to side. If he could make it to Carlisle before the snow started, he'd consider it a win.

CHAPTER TWENTY-FOUR

Mrs. Antolini turned out to be a talker. A widow, whose children and grandchildren were scattered across the mid-Atlantic region, she was eager for company. She insisted on brewing a pot of coffee for her detective guests and served the hot beverages with homemade pizzelle cookies she'd made over the weekend.

On the one hand, Burton mused, as he munched on a crisp corner of an anise-flavored snowflake, they had work to do. On the other, Mrs. Antolini's hospitality beat the dickens out of scrabbling around an abandoned house in the dark. Judging by Chrys' blissful expression as she sat beside him on the plastic-covered loveseat, he wasn't alone in his view.

Just as he was about to steer the conversation away

from Mrs. Antolini's granddaughter's success as a multi-level marketer of essential oils, he was distracted by the sight of his partner dunking her cookie into her coffee. What kind of savage would ruin a perfectly crunchy pizzelle by making it soggy?

Oblivious to her error, Chrys leaned forward, "So, Mrs. Antolini, do you know where Anastasia's living now? Or maybe where she works?"

The woman shook her head. "I'm afraid I don't. After her mother died,"—she interrupted her explanation to cross herself—"Anastasia stayed another couple months then moved out and put the house on the market. It sat empty until Damon came home from the Army and then ... after he killed that woman, it was empty again. She hasn't been back. Not once in seven years. And, no, I'm sorry, I don't know where, or if, she works. She was taking college classes when she lived here."

"Who takes care of the house?" Burton asked.

Mrs. Antolini gave a *tsk* of disapproval. "As you can see, nobody, really. Damon used to pay someone to come out and cut the grass and shovel the snow when the house was up for sale. But once the sign went down, the landscapers vanished, too. When the grass gets out of control, someone will harangue a visiting grandkid to mow it. And people take turns shoveling so the mailman doesn't break a leg."

"You could call the city, ma'am. They'll send someone out to take care of it and then bill Mr. Tenley," Chrys suggested.

The older woman sniffed. "The Kesslers may have had their problems, God rest their souls, but this isn't that kind of neighborhood."

Burton hid a smile. Murdering son or no murdering son, the good denizens of Stanton Heights weren't about to call the city on a neighbor. Time to change the subject.

"What about Olivia Scott? Anybody by that name ever stay at the house? Maybe a girlfriend of Tenley's?"

Mrs. Antolini's scowl softened. "Oh, that Olivia, she was a real sweetheart. So friendly. She moved in with Anastasia when Lisa died. She only stayed a few months to help Anastasia out. They were college classmates, if my memory's right."

"Do you remember where they took classes?"

"No. But, but Olivia works at Moretti's."

She sounded so confident that Burton wanted to believe her. "The Italian place in Bloomfield?"

"That's the one."

"You mean she used to work there?" Chrys asked.

"She still does."

"Are you sure?"

Another sniff. "Of course I'm sure. I got her the job. My maiden name is Moretti. My cousins have owned that restaurant since 1973. Olivia picked up some shifts waiting tables, and everyone loved her. She's the night manager. She's probably working tonight. Thursday's are busy, Sal and Andrea will want their best people on the floor."

Burton squeezed his fist in triumph and drained his coffee mug. "In that case, Mrs. Antolini, we'll get out of your hair. Thank you for the cookies and coffee." He stood.

Chrys followed his lead. "And the information." She scooped up the tray and the dirty dishes and carried them out to the kitchen before the woman could object.

A mere twenty-five minutes later, they'd finally managed to escape Angela Antolini, had made the seven-minute drive from her house in under five, and were parking right in front of her cousins' restaurant.

"This is a loading zone," Burton pointed out.

Chrys rolled her eyes and exited the car without responding. She hurried under the faded maroon canopy and yanked open the heavy doors. Burton trailed her at a more leisurely pace.

Inside, the dim dining room with its white tablecloths and candelabras was more than half-empty, but the lounge was crowded. Every seat at the U-shaped bar was occupied, as were most of the high tables positioned along the long wall.

A teenaged hostess appeared and grabbed two leatherette menus. "Welcome to Moretti's. Two for dinner?"

Chrys flipped her badge wallet open. "We're not dining tonight. We're looking for Olivia Scott."

The girl's eyes widened and she nodded. "I ... I'll go get her," she said as she backed away.

Burton passed the time reading the autographs on the framed celebrity photos that lined the wall. "Look, Michael Keaton ate here when he was filming *Mr. Mom*. Oh, here's the cast of *Striking Distance*. Man, I loved Dennis Farina in that, although, come on, how unbelievable was it that Bruce Willis got busted down from homicide to river rescue?" He chuckled.

Chrys shot him the rare double-raised eyebrows. "What are you going on about, old man?"

"Old man?"

"You know those movies weren't even filmed in this century, right?"

"Right. That's why they're classics."

"I don't think either film qualifies as a classic."

"Agree to disagree."

The hostess returned, hurrying to keep up with a tall brunette. She wore her hair cropped close and pinned back from her face with a pair of sparkly barrettes.

"Officers? I'm Olivia Scott, the manager here. Ashlyn said you wanted to speak to me?"

"Yes, Ms. Scott, we're detectives actually. I'm Detective Martin. This is Detective Gilbert," Chrys handled the introductions.

The young woman's smile froze on her face. "Detectives? Please don't tell me they're running drugs out of my kitchen again."

"Is there someplace private where we can talk?" Burton countered.

"Sure, follow me." She leaned over the hostess station and checked something in the reservation book, nodded to herself, and led them down a narrow hallway to a small office.

A pair of folding chairs sat across from a short desk and a third chair. The desk was flanked by two metal filing cabinets, and the room was devoid of decoration or personal touches, with the exception of a small vase that held a tight, colorful bouquet.

"Pretty," Chrys inclined her head toward the flower

arrangement.

"Thanks. On my twenty-ninth birthday I decided I was tired of waiting for a guy who would buy me flowers. So now I buy myself a bouquet every week. Forty-two weeks and counting."

"I like that." Chrys nodded approvingly.

"Look, I'm happy to help in any way I can but we do have a party of ten coming in at seven-thirty. So, not to rush you, but it would be good if we got down to business." She smiled unapologetically.

"Fair enough. We're not with the narcotics division, and our investigation doesn't involve the restaurant at all."

The young woman drew her dark brows together and pushed out her lower lip, thinking hard.

"It's about Anastasia Kessler," Chrys explained.

Olivia Scott's eyes dilated. Her nostrils flared. Her chest rose. All signs of surprise. Either she was a good actress or she was astonished.

"Anastasia? Is she okay?"

"We don't know. We can't find her," Burton said.

She nodded, knowingly. "That sounds right."

"What do you mean?" Chrys asked.

"I haven't seen her or heard from her since 2012. She ghosted."

"Can you walk us through your relationship? Start

with how you came to know her and take us through her disappearance."

"Sure, but ... why are you guys looking for her now, after all this time?"

Burton and Chrys shared a meaningful look. They had no obligation to tell this woman a blessed thing. But sometimes it paid to be friendly. They'd likely gain more cooperation, more easily, and more quickly, if they gave her something. Burton blinked at Chrys, who tilted her head.

Olivia smirked. "Do you two have a secret nonverbal language or something?"

"Something like that," Burton told her. "To answer your question, Detective Martin here and I are on the homicide squad."

Her lips parted. "Homicide? Is she ...?"

Chrys shook her head. "We don't think so. But you may have heard her brother's been in the news again."

"Sure, something about the husband of that woman he killed? But he's still in prison. Right?"

"He is. So, you were friends with Anastasia when her brother killed Raina Noor?"

"Sort of. I mean, if you'd have asked me then, I'd have said we were friends. But apparently, we weren't as close as I thought." Her voice was flat—a denial of an old hurt's ability to cause her new pain.

"Why don't you start at the beginning?" Chrys suggested in a gentle tone.

"Sure. Okay. I met Anastasia during our sophomore year at Pitt. Right before Halloween, her dad got sick, and she ended up taking a few semesters off to help take care of him. After he died, she came back for almost an entire year. But then her mom got cancer. She took off most of 2011. When her mom died, she came back again. I was finishing up my senior year. After graduation, I stuck around Pittsburgh, looking for a position with a corporation that wanted to hire an American history major. Spoiler—there weren't any. She asked me if I wanted to stay with her, rent-free, at her parents' house."

"So you moved in?"

"Yeah. And, actually, that's how I ended up working here. The next-door neighbor, Mrs.—"

"We met Mrs. Antolini. She told us all about it."

Olivia tossed her head back and laughed. "I'll bet she did. She loves to talk."

Chrys and Burton joined in with their own laughter. "Yeah, she does."

When Olivia caught her breath, she said, "But it's worked out great for me. The Morettis treat me really well. They're paying for me to go to business school."

"Nice."

"Yeah." She checked the time on her bracelet wristwatch. "So, anyway, I moved in and tried to help Anastasia get back into the swing of things at school and gave her a hand with clearing out the house and getting it ready to sell."

"Sounds like you were a good friend to her."

"I tried to be."

"But?" Chrys prompted.

She shrugged. "She had a lot going on. She had this sort of pathetic crush on one of our professors—Professor Noor, actually. You know, the one whose wife her brother killed."

Adrenaline zinged down Burton's back. "She had a thing for Giles Noor? And she told you this?"

"No, she never said a word. But it was so obvious. It was cringy, the way she fawned all over him."

Chrys scribbled something in her notebook. Then she said, "How'd she react when Mrs. Noor was killed? And then when the news came out that the murderer was her own brother?"

"I have no idea. She got sick, really sick, over the summer before she would've started her senior year. She was taking another leave of absence that fall when Damon murdered Professor Noor's wife."

"What was wrong with her?"

"She had leukemia. She started really aggressive

chemotherapy right before classes started. We'd moved out of the house by then. She was staying in a one-bedroom close to the cancer center. By then, I'd started working here and moved into a house with some girls over on Friendship Avenue."

She stopped, removed her hairpins, and raked her fingers through her hair. "I know it sounds like I was a bad friend. I tried to be there for her. I really did. I stopped by her apartment a couple times a week to bring her magazines and ice cream and hang out to keep her company, you know?"

"We're not judging you, Ms. Scott," Burton assured her.

"I guess I'm judging myself. I've always felt guilty—like I could've done more."

"Don't beat yourself up," Chrys told her.

Olivia shook her head. "I guess. Anyway, I don't know what happened to her. The last time I went by to see her, she told me her brother had left the Army. Retired, or something. And he was coming back home. He was going to donate bone marrow for her."

"Bone marrow?"

"Right. The cancer doctors basically wiped out her cells with the chemo and radiation. Then they transplanted Damon's bone marrow or stem cells—I'm not sure, I don't know the details. She was in a really hopeful mood about it. The transplant was scheduled for later that week. But when I went to see her the day before the operation, she was gone. The apartment was empty. I never saw her again. I tried to call her, but her cell phone number was disconnected."

"Did you find that strange?" Chrys asked.

"Well, yeah. Don't you?" she countered.

"Anastasia's crush on Professor Noor—how serious would you say it was?" Burton asked.

"She was pretty obsessed."

"Obsessed enough to pay her brother to kill the professor's wife?"

"Wait. What? You think Anastasia arranged the whole thing?"

"Do you think she was capable of it?"

Olivia thought for a moment. "Maybe. I know that sounds absurd. But she was in a pretty bad place. Both of her parents were dead. She was seriously ill. And she was pretty much alone in the world. Yeah. She might've been desperate enough to do something like that." She covered her mouth with her hands as if she could take back the words.

They gave her a moment to wrestle with her emotions. Then Burton said, "Do you have any pictures of Anastasia?"

"Sure, loads."

"Can we see some?"

"Well, yeah, but they're not on this phone. I'll have to go through my cloud storage. Or I might have one as the screensaver on my old iPhone. I can check when I get home tonight."

Chrys handed her a business card. "Please text any pictures you find to this number as soon as you can."

"Sure thing."

"Thanks for your help, Ms. Scott. We appreciate your time." Burton stood.

"Do you mind if I don't walk you out? I have some last-minute details to take care of before the private party gets here."

"No problem. Good night," Burton said.

Chrys stopped in the doorway and turned around. "So you really never saw her or heard from her again?"

"Never. You know, I thought I saw her once in Shadyside, going into an antique store. I even called her name. The woman turned around and looked right through me like I wasn't there." She shrugged. "Silly, huh?"

"I don't think it's silly at all. Don't forget those pictures, okay?" Chrys said.

"I won't." She repinned her hair and nodded goodbye as they walked out of her office.

CHAPTER TWENTY-FIVE

Bodhi circled Carlisle's town square, driving slowly as he scanned the streets for a parking space. He passed by the old county prison, the castle-like structure that now housed the crime lab. He found a spot across the street in front of a deli that was closed for the night.

He grabbed his backpack, waited for a break in the flow of traffic, then crossed the street against the streetlight. A light, wet snow was falling. The cold flakes on his face refreshed him, reinvigorating him from the long drive.

The historic building was surrounded by a black wrought iron fence. As he'd promised, Jim had left the gate unlatched. Bodhi latched it behind him and hurried up the steps to the arched entranceway. Before he could ring the buzzer, Jim's face appeared on the other side of the glass in the brightly lit lobby. He waved and pushed the door open, ushering Bodhi inside.

"Bodhi, good to see you! Get in here out of the weather."

"Hi, Jim."

They shook hands, and Jim hustled him further into the building. The halls were dim, lit by the emergency lighting only. "I turned on the lights in the lab, but ...." He waved a hand.

"Sure. No worries."

Jim paused at the elevator bank. "We're only one floor up. You mind taking the stairs?"

"Not at all. I could use to stretch my legs after the drive."

They started walking again. Jim pushed open a metal door and they took the flight of stairs in silence. Their footsteps cracked against the tile and echoed in the silent stairwell. They emerged on the second floor and made their way to a glass-walled laboratory that was lit up from within.

Jim used a keycard to unlock the double doors and held the door for Bodhi.

The lab looked more or less like every other forensics laboratory Bodhi had set foot in—sterile, tidy, and cold.

"Where is it?" He scanned the large room, looking for something out of place.

"The machine? It's got its own office. Well, it was a supply closet. But now, we keep the rapid DNA machine in there."

"Why?"

Jim shrugged. "Above my pay grade, friend."

"Fair enough."

Bodhi followed Jim to a door set into the wall in the back of the room. Jim opened it to reveal a surprisingly sizeable space. Inside, a sturdy table held a squat, chunky device that resembled a desktop printer. A display panel set into the front was awake and ready to go. A computer monitor and keyboard sat to the left of the device, with the hard drive tucked under the table on the floor.

Jim patted the side of the machine. "Here she is," he said fondly.

"It's smaller than I imagined."

"Yeah. If you're accustomed to the traditional machines, she doesn't look like much." Jim's pride gave way to a serious expression. "So, what do you need to run?"

Bodhi swiveled his head around and spotted a box of latex gloves on a set of wire shelves. "Do you mind if I glove up? I've already touched the sample, but it never hurts to take precautions, right?"

Jim chuckled. "Ah, you're like me. Old school. He lifted the box and held it out so Bodhi could select a pair of gloves, then plucked out a pair for himself.

As they snapped the gloves on, Bodhi said, "Is there anything else we need to do?" Tory wore a surgical face mask as well as gloves and booties when she processed DNA evidence.

Jim shrugged, "The manufacturer says no, but then, I guess you know there's some controversy about using these machines to process crime scene evidence. It's not designed for samples with multiple sources of DNA."

He nodded. "I understand. This isn't a crime scene sample. I have more of a preliminary identification situation."

Jim smiled, relieved. "Good. Buccal samples are best. Did you bring a cheek swab?"

Bodhi hated to ruin the man's night. "Sorry. I wish I did. What I have is tears. On a linen cloth." He reached into his backpack and removed the tamper-proof clear plastic evidence bag that held his handkerchief.

"Tears? I dunno ..."

"It's worth a shot. I'm prepared to accept a bad result —an unreadable sample or whatever. I'll pay for the cartridge no matter what."

Jim shook his head. "It's not that. The process destroys the sample. If this doesn't work, the sample's gone forever."

Bodhi thought for a minute. "How big of a sample does the machine need?"

"Miniscule. A scrap of material."

"So, we'll cut off one corner. I'll have the rest of the cloth. The subject more or less soaked the thing with tears."

"A real crier, huh?"

Bodhi thought back to Hope Noor's sobbing as her shoulders shook. "She was pretty upset."

A stab of regret pierced his chest. She'd been so distraught. It had seemed genuine and had stirred a well of empathy and compassion within him.

So, maybe the results will rule her out. You have to be sure.

"Okay. Let me get you a scalpel."

Jim headed out to the main laboratory, leaving Bodhi alone with his thoughts. He wasn't sure if he wanted to prove his hunch right or wrong. But he'd come this far, he needed to plow forward.

Jim returned and handed him a sterile tray that held the sharp cutting instrument. "You should do the honors."

Bodhi ripped open the bag and shook the handkerchief out onto the tray. He picked up the scalpel and bounced it against his palm lightly, getting used to its weight and feel. Then with a quick, expert motion, he sliced off one corner of the cloth.

Jim tore open a package and removed a clear cartridge roughly the size and shape of a digital thermometer. He used a pair of tweezers to pick up the sample and shove it into a channel on the side of the cartridge. He closed the compartment with a snap.

"Now what?"

"Now we feed it into the machine and wait ninety minutes."

"That's it?"

"That's it."

"Clarke's Third Law in action, huh?"

The older man chuckled. "What is it again, 'any reasonably advanced technology is indistinguishable from magic'?"

"That's the one."

"Grab a new evidence bag from the shelf for the rest of your hankie."

"You sure?"

"We aren't *that* frugal. Those bags are, what, twenty-five bucks per carton of a thousand?"

"Something like that." He used the tweezers to drop

the handkerchief into a fresh bag and sealed it. "Thanks."

He watched as Jim pressed his thumb against a small square fingerprint reader set under the LCD screen on the machine and punched in a series of numbers printed on the side of the cartridge. Then he fed the cartridge into a slot at the top of the machine. The cartridge fit in snuggly. The process reminded Bodhi of using a credit card in a machine equipped with a chip reader.

A rotating ring of circles appeared on the screen.

"It's reading it," Jim told him.

They watched in silence until the circles disappeared, replaced by a large number ninety.

"Now what?"

"Now we wait. That's a countdown timer. The numbers will tick down until we've got a result."

Bodhi stared at the machine for a moment longer then turned to Jim. "Can I buy you a cup of coffee while we wait?"

"I can't leave the machine unattended. But, no worries, the missus packed me a thermos. Pull up a chair."

An hour and a half later, Bodhi and Jim were finishing up a game of rummy when the rapid DNA machine dinged. They finished the hand and packed up the playing cards.

Then Jim popped the cartridge out of the machine and disposed of it.

"Did it work?" Bodhi asked, watching from behind Jim's shoulder. He imagined the big green check mark in the middle of the screen was a good sign.

"Yep, the processing was successful. That means the machine didn't kick the sample because it had too many different sources of DNA or too little genetic material to process. Next, the machine will connect to the CODIS database. Unless ... you said this is an identification sample. Do you have any reason to believe you'll get a hit if we search CODIS for a match? I mean, if you don't mind my asking."

Jim hadn't made any effort to pry details from him during their ninety-minute wait. They'd drunk their coffee, played cards, and talked sports, books, and movies. Bodhi had been pleasantly surprised. Law enforcement officers were some of the worst gossips he'd ever met—and he included forensic investigators and pathologists in that category. But Jim had seemed willing to remain in the dark.

His question was a reasonable one. And he'd given up his evening to help Bodhi without hesitation. The least Bodhi could do was to give him the broad strokes of his theory.

"I wish I could give you a yes or no answer. But I don't think it's that simple. The sample was taken from a woman with no known criminal record. I wouldn't expect CODIS to find a match. But, I have a suspicion that if we run it through the database, we'll get a hit."

"What? You think she assumed someone else's identity?" Jim asked.

"No. I think she has someone else's DNA. I *think* CODIS would spit out the name Damon Tenley, a convicted murderer currently serving a life sentence in the state system."

Jim's caterpillar eyebrows crawled up his forehead. "How? Only identical twins share DNA. And you can't have a male/female identical twin pair. Oh ... you think this woman had sex reassignment surgery? You know, like Bruce Jenner—I mean, Caitlyn Jenner?"

"That's a good guess, but no. There's another way two people could share DNA. Have you ever heard of a chimera?"

Jim thought. "In Greek mythology, sure. It's a fire-breathing monster with the tail of a dragon, the body of a goat, and the head of a lion." He flashed a sheepish smile. "I'm a mythology buff."

"A mythology buff with a good memory. In fact, the chimera appears in the mythologies of several cultures. The creatures differ from story to story as to which beasts and animals make up their composite parts, but the one constant is the chimera is a hybrid made up of multiple animals."

"But, your sample had a single source of DNA."

"Yeah. If I'm right, and the DNA is a match with Mr. Tenley's, I'm going to need one of the medical examiner's DNA experts to help me understand what might have happened."

"You mean you haven't already talked to the DNA scientists?" Jim gave him a bewildered look.

Bodhi laughed. "There's a saying attributed to a rear admiral in the Navy who was also a computer programming pioneer in the 1940s and 50s. She used to say—"

"It's easier to ask forgiveness than to get permission," Jim finished, shaking his head. "It's true enough. But if you make a practice of it, it can be career limiting."

"I'm retired, remember? I don't have a career to limit." Bodhi smiled. "But, to answer your question, I don't need to upload the sample to CODIS. We have a reference sample in house back in Pittsburgh. Can you email the results to this address?" He lifted the napkin from under his coffee mug and scribbled Tory's email address on it.

"Sure thing."

"Thanks."

Jim dragged his chair over to the computer keyboard and started clacking away at the keys while Bodhi stepped out into the main laboratory to call Tory Thurmont and ask forgiveness.

———

"Hello?"

Bodhi exhaled in relief. Tory sounded wide awake. He'd been worried that she might be an early to bed, early to rise type.

"Hi, Tory. It's Bodhi King."

"Bodhi? How'd you get this number?"

"Saul gave it to me. I'm sorry to bother you after hours, but I need your help."

"Is it about Tenley?"

"Yes. I have a theory about how his DNA ended up at the scene."

"Let's hear it." Her voice vibrated with anticipation.

"I think Hope Noor, Giles' wife, is a chimera."

There was a long silence. "I'm not sure I'm following."

"You know about chimerism, though, right?"

After another lengthy pause, Tory spoke again, choosing her words with obvious care. "Sure. Sometimes a twin died in the womb. It's called vanishing twin syndrome. And there's evidence that the surviving twin absorbs or somehow acquires the other twin's genetic code. There's also evidence that a woman who's given birth somehow retains bits of the embryo's unique genetic material after giving birth. But neither of those circumstances exists here. Damon Tenley was an orphaned only child, remember?"

"You're right. But the family who took him in had a daughter. She developed leukemia as a young woman, and, according to Mr. Tenley's attorney, she underwent a bone marrow transplant using stem cells harvested from Damon Tenley's bone marrow."

"Wait. Damon Tenley was a bone marrow donor?"

"According to his lawyer. And she'd have no reason to lie about it."

"Hmm. And how's Hope Noor involved?"

"Detectives Martin and Gilbert interviewed a friend of Tenley's who mentioned his sister. The girl he grew up with was named Anastasia Kessler, and she's apparently vanished from the face of the earth."

"O-kay?"

"I paid a visit to Hope Noor today. She mentioned having battled leukemia in the past."

"Wait. You think Hope Noor is Anastasia Kessler?"

"Possibly."

"Based on the fact that she and Damon Tenley's sister both had leukemia?"

"Well ... yes."

"That's pretty thin."

"Agreed. But think it through. If, *if*, Giles Noor's wife was transplanted with Damon Tenley's DNA, it would explain why his genetic material was in Giles Noor's bedroom and in such copious quantities."

"It would explain the anomalous result, but, Bodhi, that would be an extraordinary coincidence if the recipient of stem cells donated by Raina Noor's murderer ended up marrying Giles Noor."

"Unless it wasn't a coincidence at all."

"Pardon?"

"Someone paid Damon Tenley to get Raina Noor out of the way ..."

"And you think that someone was Hope or Anastasia or whatever her name is?"

"His lawyer said Damon was very protective of her. I think he would've done anything to help her."

Tory blew out a long breath. "Well, I hate to burst your speculative bubble, but there's zero actual evidence to support any of this. I know Saul admires your outside the box ideas, but, honestly, Bodhi, this one's ... a bridge too far, you know?"

Bodhi heard footsteps behind him and turned to see Jim giving him the thumb's up signal.

"There should be evidence in your email in-box right now. I lent Hope Noor a handkerchief today to wipe her eyes. A friend of mine just ran her tears through a rapid DNA machine and emailed you the results."

"What? I'm not aware of any office in the county that has a rapid DNA machine."

"Me neither. I'm in Carlisle."

"You drove to Carlisle on a hunch?"

"It's a strong hunch."

"You ... there's no chain of evidence ... the results won't be admissible ... this is ...." She was spiraling.

"If I may make a suggestion? Take a slow breath. Rapid DNA results are sanctioned, even by the most conservative voices, as appropriate for investigative purposes. If the results rule out the grieving widow, then there's no harm, no foul. But if the results come back as a match or partial match for Tenley, we can go to the district attorney and the homicide squad and share what we know. They can take it from there. Okay?"

He knew her scientific curiosity would override her concerns. Or he thought he knew as much.

Finally, after an interminable wait, she issued a grudging response. "Okay."

"Great. Can you do me a favor?"

"That depends on the favor."

"I'm going to get on the road shortly. I won't get back until close to two in the morning—"

"You should plan on getting in later than that. The snow's coming down pretty hard now."

He stifled a groan. "Right. So, I'd love to present the DNA results to Saul in the morning. Would you be willing to hop online and do some research about post-transplant chimerism in leukemia patients, and also the presence of donor DNA in human tears?"

"Sure. I'll email you any articles or studies I think are useful and you can take a look at them after you get a few hours' sleep."

"Thanks, Tory. I owe you one."

"You really do."

"I'll look for your email in the morning. When you get into the office, keep an eye out for an email from a gentleman named Jim Shore with the Cumberland County Bureau of Justice."

"Will do. I'll get in early to compare the results to my samples. Let's plan to put our heads together at eight o'clock. That way, if we need to go to Saul, we can catch him before the office starts buzzing."

"Sounds good."

"And Bodhi?"

"Yeah?"

"Drive carefully."

"I will." He was touched by her concern.

"Good. Because if you drive off the road and kill yourself, I'll be stuck holding the bag for your hare-brained idea."

He was still laughing when she hung up.

CHAPTER TWENTY-SIX

H ope slept well, better than she'd slept in weeks, and woke early, feeling refreshed and determined. She showered, packed a weekend bag and all the cash she had on hand, and went downstairs to rummage around in the refrigerator for a fast breakfast. She grabbed a container of yogurt.

She sat at the breakfast bar and ate quickly. After she rinsed the empty container and tossed it into the recycling bin, she washed and dried the spoon. Then she turned out the kitchen light and opened the door to the basement, leaving the door ajar behind her.

Her heart hammered in her chest and her legs felt like they were encased in cement as she clomped down the stairs. At the bottom of the stairs, she reached up and yanked on the chain to illuminate the bare bulb hanging above her head.

Then she crossed the earth floor and stood in front of her mother's trunk. She pressed her lips shut and folded her hands together to still their shaking. Once she was sure her emotions were contained, she lifted the hinged lid and crouched by the side of the trunk.

She moved aside the blankets and removed the pile of photo albums. She selected the bottom album and flipped it open to a picture of her as a five-year-old. She was wearing a leotard and tutu and clutched a bouquet of flowers to her chest with a proud smile. She remembered how excited she was for her first ballet recital. She reached behind the photograph and removed her old driver's license from the plastic sleeve. She slipped the ID into the pocket of her jeans and closed the picture album, resisting the urge to flip through its pages.

There's no time. You need to take care of things now.

She stacked the albums back in the trunk and replaced the blankets on top. Then she reached for one of the quilted circular boxes that occupied the other side of the trunk. She unzipped the lid and peeked inside. It was her pixie-cut wig. The short, dark black one.

Good enough. But better take at least one more in case you need to change your appearance again.

She never thought she'd be thankful that she'd lost

her hair during chemotherapy. But, she had an entire wardrobe of hairstyles and colors at her fingertips. She lifted two more wig boxes from the trunk and looped the handles over her wrist without looking inside. It didn't matter. She rezipped the pixie wig box and closed the trunk. She pounded up the stairs as fast as she could run and went straight into the attached garage to load the boxes and her bag into her car before she lost her nerve.

She returned to the kitchen one last time to confirm she hadn't forgotten anything. Then she checked the time. Almost seven o'clock. If she left now, she'd be there when visiting hours started.

She looked down at the Bible on the counter. Should she take it? Or leave it?

Her hand hovered over it while she debated. After a moment, she pulled her hand back. That book had caused her nothing but grief.

"Goodbye, Hope," she whispered.

CHAPTER TWENTY-SEVEN

B urton was only one-third of the way through his first coffee of the morning when his cell phone rang.

"Gilbert," he growled into the phone.

"Are you awake?" Chrys Martin asked.

She sounded entirely too chipper for the hour—and the weather. Then he remembered she lived in a condo.

"No, I'm still sleeping. Hey, does your condominium handle snow removal?"

"Well, yeah. Why?"

He padded to the front window and eyed his snow-covered driveway and sidewalk balefully. "Just wondering. What's up?"

"I got back from my run—"

"You went for a run? Outside? This morning?"

"Yes." She didn't hide her amusement. "Can I go on?"

"Sure."

"When I got back, I had a text from Olivia Scott. She sent a link to download a photo album from one of those cloud storage sites. I'm going to email it to you. Hang on."

He sipped his coffee and powered up his home computer while she hummed under her breath.

"Okay. It's on its way."

"This couldn't have waited until we got into the office?"

"After Dr. King called yesterday about the Noors' neighbor, I left word with the shift commander to send Vitanni out to re-interview the Remmy woman first thing this morning. I was wondering if we should call in and tell her to wait until we can get a set of photos printed so she can show them to Mrs. Remmy, ask if she ever saw this woman lurking around. If Anastasia Kessler did pay Tenley to kill Noor's first wife, maybe she paid someone to kill the professor. Maybe Hope Noor's in danger. I don't know."

"What about the DNA?"

Chrys sighed. "I don't know, Burton. Maybe the crime lab screwed it up. We can't do anything about the

DNA results, but we might as well chase the leads we *do* have."

"You're right. And good call ... to have Meredith Vitanni go back out and re-interview Mrs. Remmy. That was good thinking."

"Thanks."

He could hear the surprise in her voice. Maybe he should be less sparing with his praise.

His musings about his supervisory style were interrupted by a chiming sound that announced his ancient desktop had completed the startup process and successfully avoided consignment to the electronics recycling program for another day. He opened his email program and clicked on the message from Chrys.

He hovered his mouse over the link in the body of the message. "Am I gonna have to sign up with this storage site to view these pictures?"

"No, stop your grousing. She made the link unsecured. Just click it."

He clicked it. He drank his coffee and waited for the internet to work its magic. He drained the mug and rested it on top of a pile of unopened mail as a row of icons appeared on the computer monitor.

"I'm in."

He scanned the pictures. There were eight. Five of them were of Olivia Scott and another young woman.

Judging by the odd camera angle and the pursed duck lips, the pair of friends had been fond of taking selfies. The remaining three photos were of the other woman by herself—sitting on a blanket on the college campus green; raising a red Solo cup in a toast at what appeared to be a fraternity party; and the last one, looking pale and drained as she reclined on a sofa, wrapped up in a blanket.

"She must've lost her hair during chemo. She's clearly wearing a wig in some of these," Chrys remarked.

"Mmm-hmm."

He studied the pictures, paying particular attention to Anastasia Kessler's delicate bone structure, her large, almond-shaped brown eyes, and her bee-stung lips. He ignored the hairstyle. Decades of detective work and life as a man in society had taught him that a woman could entirely change her appearance by cutting or coloring her hair or wearing it up versus down, straight versus curly. He imagined Anastasia with long, wavy blonde hair.

"Well? Should I have the tech guys print out an array and send them with Vitanni? I hope she hasn't left."

He enlarged the final picture—Anastasia resting, looking frail and vulnerable—and stared at it. His pulse raced, and his blood pounded in his ears.

"Burt? Did you hear me?"

"I heard you. No, don't bother."

"Are you sure? What if Hope Noor's in danger from this woman?"

"She's not."

"How can you—?"

"Anastasia Kessler's not going to harm Hope Noor. She *is* Hope Noor."

"What?"

"The woman in these photographs was in my office on Tuesday crying about her murdered husband. And I told her Tenley's DNA was at the scene. I don't know what's going on, but we've been played."

"Son of a ..."

"Call dispatch and find out where Vitanni is. Have them send her out to sit on the Noor residence. I'll call Meghan Ford and have her call a meeting and then shovel my damn driveway. We need to talk to the entire team. Don't go to the station. Go straight to the DA's office. I'll meet you there."

"Will do. Wait."

"What?" he huffed, anxious to get moving.

"About the district attorney. I'm pretty sure Meghan leaked the Tenley story herself."

"How do you figure?"

"Well I got to thinking, who looks bad as a result of the leak?"

"The medical examiner, mainly."

"Right. And if the whole story comes out, about how the DNA was critically important in the first trial because the box of money and the towel weren't admissible because—"

"Because *we* screwed up by not getting a search warrant. Then we also look bad."

"But the district attorney's office comes out of it smelling like a rose."

He thought for a moment. "You're probably right. At her core, she's a politician, no different from any other elected official. It's all about the spin. But we can't worry about it now. We have to deal with Hope Noor or Anastasia Kessler or whatever her name is."

"Sure. I'm just saying, be careful what you tell the DA. Unless you want to hear it on Maisy Farley's morning segment."

"I gotcha. Now, go make your call. We have work to do."

CHAPTER TWENTY-EIGHT

D amon was sitting in his cell after breakfast. Just sitting and staring at the wall.

Officer O'Hagen rapped the bars with his baton. "Morning, Tenley."

He popped to his feet. "Good morning, Officer O'Hagen."

"Let's go."

He flashed the guard a mildly curious look. "Where?"

"Looks like you hit the jailhouse jackpot. Visiting hours just started, and guess who has the very first visitor of the day?"

Damon wrinkled his forehead in confusion. "Oh. Yeah. My lawyer said she was sending an investigator out to talk to me. But he's supposed to come in the afternoon." He shrugged. "I guess I'll have to shuffle all my other important appointments around on my calendar."

O'Hagen rewarded him with a laugh, but then he shook his head. "Pretty sure this isn't the investigator."

"It must be. I don't get any visitors."

"Well you got one today. I saw her myself. Short dark hair. Big eyes. Tight body. Miss Anastasia Kessler is here to see you."

Anastasia? Here?

Damon's knees wobbled, and he sank back onto the bed.

"Tenley, up! I don't have all day." O'Hagen's voice cracked like a whip.

Damon tried to return to his feet, but his legs didn't cooperate. He pressed his palms down hard against the mattress, hoping O'Hagen wouldn't notice the tremble in his hands.

A jumble of emotions bumped against each other, warring for primacy. Excitement that the day was here—a day he'd imagined so many times but never really believed would come. Fierce worry that this was no place for her: Anastasia shouldn't spend even one minute in this hellhole. And a frisson of fear that prickled under his skin. *What did she want?*

"Tenley." O'Hagen's voice held a warning.

"I'm sorry, officer. I ... I'm a little woozy."

O'Hagen's irritation slipped for a moment. "You need to go to the infirmary?"

Damon shook his head and forced back the bile that rose in his throat. "No. I'll be okay. I don't want to forfeit my visit." He pushed himself up off the bed.

Hope's mouth was dry. Her throat was even drier. Too dry to cough. The best she could manage was a soft choking sound. As she waited for the guards to bring Damon into the visiting room, she tried, without success, to work up some saliva and told herself there was no reason to be so anxious.

Damon adored her. He always had and always would.

Her parents had told her the story every year on her birthday. The day they'd brought her home from the hospital, he'd taken one look at her and fallen in love.

"Damon, meet your sister," her mother had said, gently placing Hope in his chubby five-year-old arms. "This is Anastasia Hope. She's our baby."

And Damon had gazed down at the bundled newborn for a long moment before raising his head and locking eyes with each of her parents in turn.

"No," he'd corrected them in a fierce voice, "she's my baby. I'm the big brother."

And from that moment on, Damon Tenley would have done anything for her.

She'd tested his loyalty over and over growing up. He lied to keep her out of trouble, took the blame when she misbehaved, and saved his money to buy her candy and stickers and dolls—and, later, makeup and clothes and beer.

When they were little, he was her constant playmate and her personal cheering section. And, as they grew up, he became her protector and her confidante. Even after he left home to join the army, he told anyone who would listen that his little sister was his world.

He'd proved it twice as an adult. Once, by saving her life. The healthy stem cells harvested from Damon's bone marrow replaced her depleted and destroyed cells after she'd gone through several courses of high-dose chemotherapy and radiation treatments. The second time, well ... he just wanted her to be happy.

Lost in her thoughts, she jumped when she heard Damon's name being called. She hurried to her feet and walked down a long, narrow hallway where she was met by a female corrections officer.

"Um ... I'm Anastasia Kessler," she croaked.

"Hand."

Hope blinked at the woman then stuck out her right hand as if they were about to shake.

The corrections officer quirked her mouth. "Other hand, honey. I need to check your X."

Anastasia blushed and held out her left hand, palm down, to display the X that the last officer had stamped on her skin.

"Sorry. I guess I'm nervous. It's my first time visiting my brother. I'm not sure how things work."

The guard's face softened. "You were smart to come out early, then, before it gets crowded. I just need to pass this ultraviolet light over your mark." She moved the wand over Hope's hand. "Good. You have the slip they gave you?"

Hope removed the piece of paper from her jeans pocket and held it up. "Yes."

"Go through those doors right in front of you and give that to the CO at the desk in the front of the room. Your brother will come in through a door on the other side of the desk. You'll have at least an hour to visit with him."

"Thank you. Is there anything else I need to know?"

"You can give him a hug or whatever when you see him, but don't get too touchy-feely. I know, I know, you're his sister. But you don't want to imagine some of the things I've seen." She paused to give a dramatic shudder. "If you purchased tokens out front, you can give them to him and he can get whatever he wants from the vending machines. Nobody else is here yet, but the room fills up fast, so pick an out-of-the-way table if you want to be able to talk semi-privately."

"Thanks again."

"Have a good visit."

Hope pushed open the door to the visiting room.

The room was nothing like she'd imagined. She'd expected to see rows of Plexiglas booths, like in the movies. Instead, she stepped into what appeared to be a school cafeteria. Rows of long tables ran the length of the room. A bank of vending machines lined the back wall. There was even a mural painted in a small alcove that held some child-sized tables and chairs.

The ordinariness of the room was disorienting and, ironically, almost surreal. Her mind swam, off-balance and racing, as she handed the paper to the guard at the desk.

D amon walked through the door to the visiting room and spotted Anastasia passing a slip of paper to the corrections officer at the desk. She was wearing her hair short. It looked like she'd dyed it a dark, chestnut color, closer to black than to brown. She looked sturdier and stronger than she had the last time he'd seen her. But, of course she would. It had been more than six years, and she'd been so frail then.

He crossed the room and stood awkwardly in front of her, his arms hanging limply by his sides. "Hi."

"Hi." She glanced at the guard. Then she darted closer to Damon and gave him a quick embrace.

By the time he realized she was hugging him, she'd already stepped back.

"Is everything okay?"

She smiled uncertainly and gestured toward the rows of empty tables. "Sure. Why don't we sit down and talk?"

He nodded and followed her to a table pushed into the far right corner of the room. He let her choose her seat first, and took the chair across from her. He leaned forward and studied her face.

"Is that one of your cancer wigs?" He gestured toward her head.

She blinked, startled. "Uh, yeah. Actually."

His heart hit his stomach. "Is the leukemia back?"

During the walk across the prison campus, he'd managed to convince himself that she was here to tell him a mix-up with the DNA evidence meant he might be able to get out of here. He hadn't imagined she could be bringing him bad news.

If Anastasia's blood cancer was back, who would take care of her?

He fisted his hands and dug them into his thighs to brace himself against the wave of helplessness that threatened to wash him away.

"No, Damon. It's nothing like that." She locked eyes with him for a long moment before glancing away. "I'm sorry I didn't bring money for vending machine tokens. I didn't know."

You'd know about the tokens if you'd visited even once in the past six and a half years. He pushed the thought away.

"Don't worry about it. I don't care about the tokens. It's good to see your face." He snaked out his hand and patted hers briefly, before the guard noticed.

She smiled wanly. "Yeah, yours, too. I have a problem I was hoping you could help me with."

"What do you need?" The words were out of his mouth before she finished her sentence.

"I'm in ... trouble," she dropped her voice to a whisper.

"Listen, there's a chance I might be getting out of here. I'll be able to help you with whatever it is." He tried to keep the excitement out of his voice.

She shook her head slowly from side to side and gave him a worried look. "No, Damon. You have a life sentence. I'm sorry, but you're not getting released."

"No, no. Listen. I have a meeting later today with my lawyer's investigator. That lady who we—I—killed? Someone offed her husband, and the DA says it was me." He laughed, a high-pitched nervous laugh. "How crazy is that? But it makes all their evidence against me look fishy."

Her brown eyes were stark in her white face. "You're not getting out," she repeated. Her tone was insistent, almost urgent.

Irritation flashed in his chest. "It almost sounds like the idea bothers you."

"Don't be silly. I love you. I don't want to see you rotting away in here." She gave him a tremulous smile. Then she cocked her head to the side. "But, you know, you *did* kill that woman."

His irritation swelled and then exploded.

"Are you insane? She was *obsessed* with you ... tormenting you. You *begged* me to help you. Anastasia, for crying out loud, you paid me to do it."

"Keep your voice down," she hissed. She tilted her head toward the bored guard in the front of the room.

Her sharp tone filled him with instant shame. "You're right. I shouldn't have snapped at you."

She pressed her lips together in a thin line of displeasure and nodded her agreement.

"Please, Anastasia. I'm really sorry. Will you forgive me?"

"I guess."

He exhaled in relief. "Thank you."

"You're welcome."

"So what kind of trouble are you in? How can I help from in here?"

She stared at him, her eyes boring into his. "Raina Noor, the woman who died—"

"Your stalker," he reminded her.

Raina Noor's husband was one of Anastasia's professors. For some reason, the woman had gotten it into her head that her husband was attracted to Anastasia. Which, maybe he was, but Anastasia wasn't that kind of girl. And on top of everything, she was battling leukemia. The constant accusations and confrontations were taking a toll on Anastasia's health and her mental state. She was desperate when she came to Damon for help.

"Um, yeah. So, when I was strong enough to go back to school, Professor Noor was so kind to me." Her gaze dropped to the laminated table between them and she traced circles on the surface with one finger. "After some time, we fell in love."

"You're involved with Noor?" He asked slowly.

"We got married in 2014, Damon."

His brain was bouncing off the inside of his skull. He scrabbled for a response. "Wow. Congratulations, I guess. Wait—was any of that stuff about his wife even true?"

Had he killed a woman just to get her out of Anastasia's way?

"Damon, please. He's dead ..." Tears welled in her eyes, threatening to spill over.

"I'm sorry."

"Thank you. But now you can see why you can't ask your lawyer to challenge your DNA evidence, right?"

"What? Why?"

"If your case is reopened, the police will start searching for the person who paid you all over again."

"I told you I didn't want your money. It just caused more problems."

Her eyes flashed, but she didn't argue.

"And, if you make a big stink about the DNA results from the first time, they're going to have to look closer at both cases."

"But, this is my chance to get out. Don't you understand? Do you want me to live the rest of my life like this?" He raised his hands up and looked around the room. "Here?"

She looked back at him, her face impassive. "Do you want *me* to spend the rest of my life in a place like this? Because that's what'll happen, Damon."

"But why?"

"After you were in the papers, I started using my middle name. Giles never knew you and I were connected. I couldn't tell him, obviously. But he found the family Bible, where Mom wrote your name on the line under hers and Dad's and ... he freaked out. We had a huge fight. I ... I had to protect myself."

His stomach lurched, sour and jumpy. He let out a shallow, shaky breath. "What did you do?"

Her expression hardened into a mask. "What I had to do."

He stared at her as if he were seeing her for the first time. "Anastasia, what do you want from me?" He edged his voice with steel.

Her eyes widened and her voice softened. "Damon, please ... you said you'd always be there for me."

He tried to resist, but he could feel his heart cracking open. It had been like this for his whole life. He couldn't deny her anything.

"Okay, bug. What do you need?"

She smiled at her childhood nickname. "I knew you'd help me. I love you, D."

"I know you do." She did. Even though she rarely showed it. He knew. "I love you, too. You're my world."

She walked her hand across the table and rested it on his arm. "I need you to let go of this idea about challenging the DNA. If anyone finds out I killed Giles or asked you to kill Raina, it'll ruin my life. But you're already in here. Just tell your lawyer you changed your mind."

"Anastasia—"

"For me, Damon. Please." Her eyes pleaded with him.

I can't do this anymore.

The thought reverberated inside his head. He'd made his peace with what he'd done—or thought he had. But six years on the inside was a long time. And he had another fifty or sixty to go. The chance of beating the charge was tantalizing, a temptation that he knew he'd end up giving into despite his promises to Anastasia.

He swallowed around the lump in his throat, and nodded his head. "Okay."

CHAPTER TWENTY-NINE

Bodhi was too tired to ride his bike to work. Because of the snow and a three-car pileup he got stuck behind just after the Sidling Hill Exit, the drive home from Carlisle had taken him more than four-and-a-half hours, instead of three.

So when he woke up at six-thirty, after a measly three hours' rest, he sleepwalked through his morning routine then warmed up the VW Bug while he shoveled and salted the front walk.

An hour later, he'd battled through Pittsburgh's snowy rush hour traffic and was sitting in his temporary office at the medical examiner's building, hiding a yawn behind his mug of green tea.

Tory walked into the room at eight o'clock on the

dot. Her complexion was rosy—whether the color was from excitement or the cold, Bodhi couldn't be sure.

"You were right!" she exclaimed by way of greeting, removing all doubt as to the source of her flushed cheeks. She waved a sheaf of papers at him.

He abandoned his tea, suddenly alert and clear-minded.

"I was starting to wonder. I thought you were going to email me the studies?"

She smiled guiltily. "I was. But I ended up going down a rabbit hole ... and, by that point, it was so late, I figured I'd walk you through my findings in person. But, here, these copies are for you."

"Thanks." He flipped through the studies. "Can you give me the highlights for now? We should get in to see Saul as soon as we can."

"Right. Broad strokes." She reached into the chest pocket of her lab jacket, pulled out her eyeglasses, and put them on. "Hope Noor is a chimera."

"So she has a mixture of her own original DNA and Damon Tenley's donated DNA?"

"Yes, maybe. Typically, chimerism involves mixed DNA. But her tears contained Damon Tenley's DNA *only*."

"How can that be possible?"

"Read the second study in your stack. The

researchers evaluated buccal swabs, blood samples, and hair follicle samples from peripheral stem cell and bone marrow transplant recipients, including patients with leukemia. If you look at the chart, you'll see that the leukemia patients' blood samples showed *one hundred percent* donor DNA. The hair and cheek samples were mixed."

"What about tears?"

"Yeah, so, tears aren't typically the best source of DNA. You know, the genetic material is diluted. So, I didn't find any studies that specifically used tears to confirm chimerism. But you know your source was Hope Noor or Anastasia Kessler or whoever she is. And the sample results match Damon Tenley. So it's safe to hypothesize that tears, like blood, can show complete replacement of the original DNA with donor DNA. Because it happened."

"And you'd expect to see this result more than six years post-transplant?"

"Again, I didn't find any studies that tested for chimerism that far out from transplant. But DNA can survive for years outside the body if the conditions are right. Why not inside the body, particularly a body where the original DNA has been utterly wiped out by aggressive chemotherapy and radiation?"

He nodded. "That holds water. But your Giles Noor

crime scene report said Hope Noor's DNA was also found at the scene. How? And how did you match it?"

"Dried sweat on the bed sheets came back with three sources of DNA. We matched Tenley in the CODIS database and Giles against his corpse. That left one unknown. Standard procedure would be to get a sample from everyone in the household, which meant Hope. She was a mess, practically catatonic, the night of the murder. So I told Fred to ask her for a hair sample. Less invasive, quicker, and less messy. She consented, and he plucked five strands from her head."

"And donor DNA isn't always found in hair follicles—"

"More often than not, at least in leukemia patients, the percentage of donor DNA is insignificant, according to the study."

"So you matched the sweat DNA to the hair DNA without realizing Hope Noor's sweat contained her DNA as well as her donor's."

"Exactly."

"So ..."

"So ..."

"Anastasia Kessler, also known as Hope Noor, killed Giles."

"I feel like I screwed up. I didn't even consider chimerism."

He searched her tight, tense face. "And there's no reason why you would. Chimerism is an anomalous event. A convicted murderer acting as a bone marrow donor for someone who will later commit a murder of her own is a one-of-a-kind event. That just doesn't happen, Tory."

She barked out a tight laugh. "Well, when you put it that way ..."

"Exactly. And you have neither the time nor the budget to treat every sample as an outlier. Saul would have your head if you did."

This time her laugh was genuine. "Speaking of Saul, we need to bring him up to speed."

A voice broke into their conversation. "Not right now. We've been summoned to the DA's office. Stat."

They turned in unison to see Saul standing in the door with a grim expression.

"You drive," Bodhi told him. "We'll fill you in on the way."

CHAPTER THIRTY

"I t's your party, detectives. Take it away," Meghan said once the entire group was assembled around her office's largest conference room table for the third time in less than a week. She waved a hand toward Detectives Gilbert and Martin.

To Bodhi's moderate surprise, Detective Martin took the lead. "Thanks, Meghan. We asked the district attorney to call this last-minute meeting because there's been a development in our investigation. Detective Gilbert and I appreciate everyone making room in their schedules on no notice."

Saul interjected, "You had great timing, actually. On the drive over, Dr. King and Ms. Thurmont filled me in on a development on our end, so we're going to need a few minutes of everyone's time after the detectives have finished."

Roland Lee laughed. "It looks like I'm the only one without big news." He shot Meghan a sideways look as he said it, and Bodhi suspected Roland didn't fully trust his boss.

"Why don't I get started then?" Detective Martin took a stack of photo prints out of a folder and handed them to Tory, who was on her left. "Take one and pass the rest, if you don't mind."

Tory removed the top print and handed the stack to Bodhi. As Bodhi passed the pictures to Saul, he studied the sheet in his hand. Three photographs were arrayed on the page. Three haunted-looking women stared back at him. No, wait. One woman, three different hairstyles. Something about the curve of her lips and the shape of her large eyes resonated, striking a chord in his memory.

He looked up at Detective Martin as the pictures made their way around the table. "Is this ... ?"

"Hope Noor. Yes. Also known as Anastasia H. Kessler, daughter of Frank and Lisa Kessler, who were Damon Tenley's guardians after his parents died. She grew up considering Tenley her older brother. We assume"

"How?" Meghan demanded. "How did Giles Noor

end up married to the sister of the man who killed his first wife?"

Detective Gilbert fielded the question. "Interview subjects paint a picture of a close relationship between Anastasia/Hope and Tenley. It also appears she had a crush on Professor Noor. It's possible she's the one who paid Tenley to get Raina Noor out of the way so she could make a move on him."

"If that's true, she's as demented as Tenley is," Roland observed.

"No argument from me," the detective responded.

"Okay, assuming for the sake of argument that Tenley killed Raina at Hope's request, that still doesn't explain why his DNA was present when Giles was murdered more than six years later," Meghan said.

"Bodhi and Tory have a theory about that," Saul offered.

Tory caught Bodhi's eye and mouthed 'you do it.' He turned to Detective Martin. "Should I jump in now?"

"Sure."

"Anastasia Kessler was diagnosed with leukemia at some point in 2011 or 2012. Mr. Tenley was tested to see if he could donate bone marrow or peripheral stem cells—"

"What's the difference?" Roland wanted to know.

"For our purposes, there isn't one. Both procedures are referred to under the general umbrella of a 'bone marrow transplant.' The harvesting process differs, but the result is the same. The transplant recipient receives healthy donor white blood cells to replace the cancerous blood cells, which have been wiped out by chemo-therapy, irradiation, or a combination of the two."

"And Tenley was a match?"

"Yes, according to his lawyer."

Meghan narrowed her eyes. "You've been talking to Penny Geoffries?"

Before Bodhi had the chance to respond, Detective Martin interjected. "That squares with what Anastasia's former roommate and Tenley's old army buddy both told us. She had leukemia, and Tenley donated his bone marrow."

"And this happened before Raina Noor's murder?" Meghan asked.

"Yes. I don't know the exact timing, but it was some-where in the neighborhood of three to six weeks before Raina was killed," Bodhi confirmed.

"Okay. Go on."

"Although we think of a person's DNA as being as unique as a snowflake—or better yet, a fingerprint, that's not always true."

"You mean like in the case of identical twins?"

Detective Gilbert asked.

"Yes, or in this case, when a transplant recipient receives stem cells from a donor. That donor's DNA is encoded in the cells. So, now, she has both sets of DNA in her body. It's called chimerism."

Both prosecutors and both detectives stared hard at Bodhi, Tory, and Saul.

"This is a real thing?" Roland Lee wanted to know.

"It's real, and Bodhi called in a favor with another jurisdiction to use a rapid DNA machine to confirm that Hope Noor is carrying Damon Tenley's DNA. I reviewed the results myself," Tory said.

There was a heavy silence.

"So, is our theory that the wife killed Giles Noor?" Meghan asked.

"That's the medical examiner's current working hypothesis," Saul said. He looked at Detective Gilbert.

"The PPD is operating under the same theory."

"Well, hell. What's her motive?"

"Apparently, the Noors had an argument the night Giles was killed. We sent a uniform out to re-interview a neighbor about the fight and to see if she could identify Hope as Anastasia from the photos. I guess there's no need to get the ID seeing as how the ME's office has DNA confirmation," Detective Gilbert said.

"Do we know where Hope Noor is right now?" Meghan asked.

"No, but I told Vitanni to sit on the Noor house when she finishes taking the witness statement. I'll call her now to tell her to skip the photo identification," Detective Martin offered. She stood and walked over to the windows at the far side of the room to make the call.

"Do we have enough for an arrest warrant?" Detective Gilbert asked.

Meghan frowned. "Possibly. But given the optics, I'd like to get a search warrant for the house and her vehicle first and see if we can find more to connect Hope Noor to Anastasia Kessler. Write it up yourself and run it by Roland before you take it to a judge."

Detective Gilbert scowled back at her. "With all due respect, I don't need a prosecutor to babysit me on a search warrant."

The district attorney arched a brow. "After what happened during the Tenley search, I'd like you to humor me."

"You should include the family Bible as an item on the warrant. I found it in the kitchen, mixed in with a stack of cookbooks. I assumed it belonged to Hope because Giles was Jewish. At the time, I thought it was just out of place. But it could have been hidden," Bodhi said in a low voice to Detective Gilbert.

The detective nodded. "Most family Bibles have a space where you can keep handwritten family records—births, deaths, marriages. If Anastasia Kessler's or Damon Tenley's name is in that book, it'll go a long way to proving the connection."

Detective Martin ended her phone call and returned to the table.

"The neighbor told Officer Vitanni the Noors had a screaming match Tuesday evening. Her windows were closed because of the cold, of course, but when she went down to the curb to get her recycling bin and bring it back to the house, she heard Hope shouting about Giles' obsession with the past. Giles in turn told Hope he didn't even know who she was."

"Good thing Mrs. Remmy chose that precise moment to retrieve her recycling bin," Detective Gilbert deadpanned.

"Isn't it, though? She also said that she saw Hope leave the house early this morning. Around seven A.M. She hasn't returned. Mrs. Remmy invited Vitanni to keep watch from her living room window until Hope comes back."

If she comes back, Bodhi thought.

Now where did that notion come from?

He wasn't sure. But if Hope suspected they were

getting close to her, she seemed like the type who might take off.

His cell phone vibrated in his pocket. He pulled it out and saw a text notification. He held the phone under the edge of the table and opened his texting app. The message was from Maisy, and it was short:

Damon Tenley is dead. Call me when you can.

CHAPTER THIRTY-ONE

"Maisy, what happened?"

"Now, is that anyway to greet a friend, sugar?" Maisy drawled.

Bodhi could tell her heart wasn't in it, but he played along.

"I'm sorry, Maisy. I didn't mean to be rude. I just was so shocked when I got your text that I forgot my manners."

"Well, that's understandable. Isn't it *awful?*"

"What happened?" he repeated.

Maisy sighed. "I really wish Penny would just tell you herself, but she insisted she can't call you, because y'all are on opposite sides. So, if I get any details mixed up, don't you go blaming me."

"I won't," he promised. As if there was any chance

the tough-as-nails investigative reporter hidden within Maisy's sugar cookie exterior would get her facts wrong.

"Penny's investigator, Kell, was supposed to go to the prison this afternoon to meet with Damon. Apparently, scheduling legal team visits sometimes goes all wonky, so Kell called out to Fayette this morning to confirm everything and make sure he didn't drive all the way out there only to find out there was no meeting room set aside or something like that."

"Okay."

"Well, he got transferred around a bunch, and they finally connected him with Warden Hardiman himself who said Damon Tenley hanged himself in his cell less than an hour ago."

"He committed suicide?"

"Mmm-hmm. Now, according to Penny, Kell pushed the warden pretty hard on that fact, and he insisted it was suicide."

"Why would he kill himself now? It may be a long shot, but there's a chance his sentence could be overturned."

"Which is exactly what Kell said. So, Kell went and got Penny and they both talked to the warden who told them ...." She paused dramatically.

Bodhi waited in silence.

"Oh, you're no fun. You could beg me to tell you,

you know. Fine. The warden said Damon Tenley had a visitor first thing this morning. You'll never guess who it was."

"Anastasia Kessler."

"Grr, you really *are* no fun. How'd you know?"

"Lucky guess."

"Warden Hardiman says she's never visited Damon before, but the corrections officer who escorted him back to his cell reported that he was in decent spirits. Maybe a little quiet, is all. And then a guard came to take him to class—he was taking business courses—and he was swinging from the ceiling or whatnot. It's just terrible."

"It is. It's tragic. Will you let Penny know we're getting very close to finding out what happened with his DNA and I'm not gonna stop until we have answers? It would mean a lot if you could tell her."

"Well, I suppose I can't say no, now can I? I can't believe y'all are acting exactly like a pair of junior high kids passing messages through a third party. Ask him if he likes me? Why, does she like me? Don't tell her I wanted to know."

"It's not *exactly* the same. But I appreciate the help."

"Mmm-hmm. Well, here's another little nugget of assistance, just between the two of us. You know I ordinarily wouldn't divulge a source, but my DNA tip came from Meghan Ford. She's apparently considerin' a run for judge and wants to make her office look good."

Meghan? Her anger over the leak had all been for show? What a monumental waste of the team's time.

"That's interesting."

"Interesting? No, it's infuriating. I do *not* enjoy being manipulated." Maisy's temper flared, which had the unexpected effect of flattening her Southern accent.

"That's fair."

"Oh, Meghan has no idea what she's started. I got a *very* interesting call from Annette Morris, who used to work in the prosecutor's office and heard about the new issue concerning Damon Tenley's DNA. Now, Annette told me Meghan made her play a little loose with the evidence during the original trial—to the point that she started looking for jobs as soon as it ended."

"Did Ms. Morris share any specifics about how Meghan pressured her?" He was thinking of Tory, and the testimony that had made her so uncomfortable that she'd called in sick to avoid taking the stand.

"I don't have details, but you better believe I'm gonna get them. I lost my shot at an exclusive with Damon, but his death opens up a whole new line of investigation into how and why he was railroaded."

He shook his head. "Don't get out over your skis. I'm confident he *did* kill Raina Noor."

She *tsked* at the warning. "I always stick to the truth, Bodhi. You know that."

He laughed. It was true. For all of Maisy's theatrics and drama, she was as ethical a journalist as he'd ever met.

"Well, in that case, go get 'em, tiger."

"Right back at you, my friend. Now, I gotta run and tell Penny I delivered her message. You should listen to the noon news. The public defender's office called a press conference."

Bodhi ended the call and returned to the conference room to share the news of Anastasia Kessler's visit and Damon Tenley's subsequent suicide with the team.

"Hardiman's sure it was suicide?"

"Why would Anastasia visit him *now*?"

"Do you think she knows he killed himself?"

Overlapping questions were flying at Bodhi too rapidly for him to possibly answer any of them.

Finally, Saul held up a hand.

"Listen, people. Damon Tenley's suicide is a distraction. It's theater. Our primary objectives right now should be twofold: We need to find Hope Noor/Anastasia Kessler and we need to get a judge to sign a search warrant for the Noor home. And when I say *we*, I mean *you*. Because *we*"—he paused to gesture toward himself, Tory, and Bodhi—"are forensic scientists and pathologists. So, we're going to head back to the lab. Best of luck to the rest of you."

Saul stood, and Tory and Bodhi rose to their feet as well.

Meghan spluttered. "You can't just walk out and leave this mess in my lap."

"Respectfully, Meghan, there's very little the medical examiner's office can do at this point. Other than prepare for Mr. Tenley's autopsy, assuming the Department of Corrections is going to send the body to us rather than a state police lab."

Roland Lee kept his eyes locked on his legal pad, committed to staying out of the line of fire. The homicide detectives exchanged a look. Then Detective Gilbert cleared his throat.

"Dr. David, given all this stuff about Hope Noor being a chimera, it'd be helpful to sit down with your people before I draw up the search warrant for Roland to review. Just to make sure I include everything that will help establish that she has this condition."

Roland remained fixated on his pad of paper. He didn't even glance up at the mention of his name.

"That's sensible," Saul agreed. "Why don't we walk out together? I'm sure Bodhi and Tory will make time to talk to you and Detective Martin this morning."

"Definitely," Tory chimed in.

Bodhi nodded. It would give him a chance to tell the detectives that Penny Geoffries was planning to give a press conference. That tidbit of information wasn't something he planned to share with the district attorney while she was in her current mood.

Meghan gaped at them for a nanosecond; then she clamped her mouth and turned to glare at Roland. Bodhi cast the lawyer a sympathetic look before he trailed the others out of the conference room, leaving him to his fate.

CHAPTER THIRTY-TWO

Hope was a cautious driver by nature. When she left the prison, the primary roads were cleared but the secondary roads were still snow covered. The driving conditions, coupled with the emotions that had been stirred up by seeing Damon, had the effect of making her a cautious, slow driver.

She couldn't afford to get pulled over for speeding or blowing through a red light. Not when she was this close to a fresh start. She'd leave town, at least until things settled down. Damon would keep his mouth shut. Eventually, the police would close the case and Giles' death would fade into the background.

Her heart was heavy, though. Seeing Damon in an orange jumpsuit, looking old and defeated, had hurt.

He's giving you a second—third—chance. Don't waste it.

She nodded to herself. The best way to honor Damon and thank him for his sacrifice would be to live her new life as fully and joyfully as she could. That's what he wanted for her. That's what he always wanted for her.

She merged onto the highway, headed north. She'd drive right through Pittsburgh and keep going until she picked up the turnpike in Harmarville. Once she made it to Ohio, she could stop and get some lunch. She'd unfold her map and pick a destination.

Comforted by the prospect of a plan, she loosened her grip on the steering wheel and wriggled her shoulders. Maybe some music would help lift her mood.

She shifted her eyes from the road and pressed the radio button.

"...go to live coverage of a statement from Penny Geoffries with the Allegheny County Public Defender's Office."

She rolled her eyes and changed the stations. Before she got too much further in her adventure, she'd have to update the presets. Giles and his incessant love for the news had meant that at least three of the saved stations were devoted to local news.

"—Ms. Geoffries represented Damon Tenley,

convicted murderer and the so-called Squirrel Hill Slayer who fatally beat Raina Noor to death in 2012."

Hope froze for an instant. Then she turned up the volume.

"Mr. Tenley's name came up in the investigation into Raina Noor's widower, Giles Noor, who was beaten to death in an eerily similar fashion just last week. We go live to Grant Street to hear what the public defender has to say:

"Thank you for braving the weather, folks. I'm going to read a short, prepared statement. This office represented Damon Tenley. In light of recent reports that the authorities were attempting to tie Mr. Noor's murder to my client, despite the fact that Mr. Tenley is, and has been, incarcerated in a maximum-security facility, my office was considering reopening Mr. Tenley's case. Today, Kell Berg, a senior investigator with the office, was scheduled to meet with Mr. Tenley. When he called SCI-Fayette to confirm the arrangements, he was informed that Mr. Tenley was dead. Allegedly, Damon Tenley took his own life in his cell sometime between nine o'clock and ten o'clock this morning. We're calling on the Department of Corrections and local law enforcement to undertake a thorough review of the circumstances surrounding Mr. Tenley's demise. We're also calling on the District Attorney's Office, the Medical

Examiner's Office, and the Pittsburgh Police Homicide Squad to provide an explanation for the anomalous DNA results that have been reported to the media. Thank you."

Damon's dead? Hope's head spun and her breathing grew shallow.

She'd wanted him to take the fall for her, but not like this.

That's not true, she corrected herself. *You knew you might push him over the edge when you went to see him. Plus, admit it: it's cleaner this way. With him gone, nobody's going to keep looking for his partner. You're almost home free.*

Her vision blurred, and she realized she was crying.

She steadied her hands on the wheel and blinked hard to clear away her tears.

It's going to be okay. Just stick to the plan.

She glanced up and gasped. Her entire rearview mirror was filled with the front of a tractor trailer. She gripped the wheel and squeezed her eyes shut as the truck plowed into the back of her sedan. The car spun sideways, wobbled, and careened off the road and down an embankment. It smacked off a thick tree and came to rest in a gully, just feet from the river.

The truck driver was nearly as shaken as she was. He gripped his hat in one hand and mopped the sweat from his forehead while repeatedly telling her how sorry he was.

She casually patted her hair to confirm her wig was in place then mustered a trembling smile.

"I'm okay," she assured him.

She unfastened her seat belt.

"I don't think you oughta move until the first responders get here."

"You ... called 911?" She tried to keep the anger out of her voice.

"Yes, ma'am. My truck's not damaged, but your car is about totaled. Now don't you worry, after we fill out the police reports, my home office will call your insurance company and get everything taken care of. But first thing's first, we have to get you checked out."

No. No. No.

"No."

"Pardon?"

"I can't sit here and wait." Her mind raced, searching for a reason he'd accept, and then a calm came over her. The truth. The truth would get her out of this. "I ... I just found out my brother died this morning. I *have* to get home."

She fixed her eyes on his and waited.

"Oh, man ... I'm so sorry." He jammed his hat back on his head and flapped his hands. "I don't know what to do."

"Could you give me a lift? My place is right up the hill. I'll take care of the car later."

"Uh ... what about the police report?"

"You know, with the way the roads are, it could take them a long time to get out here." She let her eyes fill. "I can't wait. Please help me."

She watched his face soften then melt.

Got him.

"Sure. Sure thing, miss."

She exhaled. "Oh, thank you."

She grabbed her bag from the back seat and hopped out of the car before he could change his mind. Detouring to her parents' old place wouldn't set her back too far, and nobody would think to look for her there. This was a solid plan B.

He held out his hand to help her up the icy hillside.

CHAPTER THIRTY-THREE

Burton was sitting at a stainless steel table in Tory Thurmont's lab. He was trying hard to focus on the DNA lesson Bodhi and Tory were giving him and Chrys. In truth, though, his eyes had glazed over sometime around the part where they'd explained the difference between autologous and allogeneic transplants and the dangers of graft-versus-host disease. He just had to hope that Chrys was paying attention.

Chrys' cell phone sounded.

"Hang on a sec, that's probably Officer Vitanni." She unlocked the screen. "Huh. No, it's dispatch." She shrugged at Burton. "This is Martin."

Burton watched as her eyes went wide and she flipped open her notebook and started scrawling notes.

"We're on our way."

She ended the call and got to her feet. Burton joined her.

"Where are we going?"

"911 got a report of an accident on Route 28 North. An eighteen-wheeler rear ended a sedan and pushed it over the embankment."

"Injuries?"

"Apparently not. The truck driver called it in. But when the paramedics arrived at the scene, the truck was gone and the sedan had been abandoned. When a traffic unit rolled up, the officers ran the plates and the car came back registered to Hope Noor."

Burton's biology-inspired drowsiness lifted and adrenaline pumped through his veins. "Where exactly did this happen?"

"Right before the ramp to the 62nd Street Bridge."

He squinted at the ceiling. "That's just down the hill from her childhood home. It's, what, a mile, a mile and a half? That's a five-minute drive, tops."

"Yeah, but her car's still in the ravine. In this weather, it would take close to an hour to walk it," Chrys pointed out.

Bodhi cleared his throat. "She got a lift from the truck driver."

"Are you psychic, now?" Chrys asked.

"I spent enough time with her to know that she's very good at appealing to a person's protective instincts. She projects a vulnerability that makes you want to help her."

"She got to me, too," Burton admitted.

Tory added, "It seemed to work on Damon Tenley, as well."

"We'll have to finish this later," Chrys said.

"May I tag along?" Bodhi asked.

"No." Chrys shook her head.

"No. You stay put." Burton jerked his head toward the door and Chrys followed him out of the room.

Bodhi and Tory sat in silence and listened to the clacking of the detectives' footsteps grow fainter as they walked down the hallway. After the chime sounded to announce the arrival of the elevator, Tory turned to Bodhi and grinned.

"Do you want to drive or do you want me to?"

He blinked at her. "Are you suggesting we ignore the homicide detectives' order to stay put?"

"Last time I checked, neither of us report to them."

"Fair point, but I don't know where Hope Noor grew up. Do you?"

"The address'll be in the Raina Noor case file. It's where Tenley was staying when they arrested him."

Bodhi considered the possible ramifications of turning up uninvited at an active crime scene. Then he returned Tory's smile. "Bring your car around. I'll dig up the address and meet you in front of the building."

She grabbed her purse, coat, and scarf and hurried out of the lab.

Bodhi turned out the lights and walked along the hallway to the small office Saul had loaned him. He paged through the Raina Noor files until he reached the police report; then he copied the defendant's address onto a sticky note and returned the files to the metal filing cabinet.

He was buttoning his coat when Saul poked his head into the office.

"Oh, are you heading out?"

Bodhi reminded himself about forgiveness, not permission. "Yes."

Saul cocked his head. "Early lunch?"

"Um, no."

They looked at one another for a long moment. Saul pursed his lips. "Hmm. Be careful ... you know, the streets might be icy."

"Right."

"Right."

"Well, I should get going." Bodhi nodded and ushered Saul out of the office. Saul shook his hand before they parted ways.

CHAPTER THIRTY-FOUR

Burton parked in an alley that ran behind the street. After some debate, he and Chrys agreed to approach the house on foot.

They climbed out of the sedan and started tromping through the slushy snow. When they reached Mrs. Antolini's back gate, he stretched out an arm and stopped Chrys.

"What?" she hissed as she bounced off his forearm.

"I have some rapport with her. I'll go to the front door and knock. You cover the back exit."

"I don't think she'll run; she'll try to talk her way out—"

"She's cornered now, Chrys. And she's probably heard by now that Damon's dead. We can't predict how she'll act."

Chrys shrugged. "Fine. We'll play it your way."

She crouched behind Mrs. Antolini's shed and checked her weapon. Burton walked to the end of the alley, turned left on the cross street, then made another left onto the Kesslers' street, and walked briskly up to the house, which, if anything, looked more dilapidated in the daylight.

He rapped on the door. No response. He knocked again, harder this time. Mrs. Antolini's face appeared in her living room window. He motioned for her to back away and thanked the stars when she did.

"Hope? Anastasia?" he called loudly. "It's Detective Burton Gilbert. I understand you've been in an accident. Are you okay?"

He listened hard but heard no movement inside.

Then, the slightest creak sounded from within the house.

He turned his ear toward the door and heard the sound of a window pane being raised on the second floor.

He stepped to the edge of the porch and craned his head back to look up. That's when he spotted the barrel of a gun protruding from an open second-story window. He dove and rolled across the porch floor until he was flush with the front wall of the structure.

She fired. The bullet struck a cement birdbath and shattered the base.

She was a lousy shot, which, unfortunately, didn't make him feel any better about his odds. A cornered, erratic woman with poor gun-handling skills was a disaster waiting to happen.

Chrys came pounding up the walkway from the back of the house, shouting his name as she ran.

"Get down!" he screamed.

She hit the ground on her belly and army crawled through the snow-covered shrubbery on her elbows. Then she crouched low and ran up the stairs to press herself up against the facade next to him.

"Why is she shooting?"

"Because she's a cornered killer. Call for backup."

"Already did. As soon as she fired the first shot."

They sagged against the house, breathing hard.

An SUV pulled up directly in front of the house and parked. Burton blinked, looked again, and swore under his breath.

"We've got company."

Chrys squinted. "Is that ... Bodhi King and Tory Thurmont?"

Bodhi ducked his head to peer through the windshield of Tory's SUV.

"Are you sure this is the right address?" Tory asked.

"It's the address that was in the file. And judging by the two homicide detectives with their guns drawn on the front porch, she's here."

Tory removed her glasses and rubbed her eyes with her fist. She replaced the glasses on her face and focused on the porch. "Oh, yeah."

"Get out of here," Detective Gilbert roared from the porch.

An instant later, the crack of a gun ripped through the air and a bullet tore into the retaining wall that fronted the yard, sending plaster and brick dust into the air like a water spout.

Tory put the SUV in reverse and backed away from the house. Another shot hit the street in front of the car.

"This may have been a bad idea," Tory said.

Before Bodhi could respond, his cell phone rang. He dug it out of his coat pocket and hit the speaker button.

"Hello, this is Bodhi King."

"Dr. King?"

He recognized the breathy voice at once. "Mrs. Noor?"

Tory's eyes widened.

"Yes. Are you in the silver SUV I just shot at?"

"Um, yes, I am."

"I thought I caught a glimpse of your hair. I didn't realize who you were until after I took a shot. I'm so sorry." Her distress sounded genuine.

"It's okay, you missed us."

"Us? Who's driving?"

"Her name is Tory Thurmont. She's a forensic serologist. She's helping me understand your condition."

"I don't have a condition. My leukemia's in remission."

Tory looked at him with a question in her eyes. He nodded to go ahead.

"Mrs. Noor? This is Tory. It seems you have what's called chimerism. In addition to your own DNA, you have Damon Tenley's DNA as a result of the bone marrow transplant you underwent."

"So ... I left his DNA in my bedroom?"

"Correct."

She paused and Bodhi could almost hear the wheels turning in her mind. After a moment, she said, "So whoever killed Giles must've worn gloves or cleaned up after himself. Because the only DNA you found was Giles', mine, and Damon's, right?"

Tory rolled her eyes. He nodded. Hope's explanation strained credulity.

But it struck him as bad form to call an armed woman a fabulist, so he cleared his throat and said, "That would be one possibility."

Bodhi heard a soft tapping sound on the side of his door. He peered down and saw Detective Martin crouched beside the quarter panel.

"It's the only possibility," Hope retorted.

'Keep her talking. We're going in,' she mouthed.

She mimed holding a phone to her ear and pointed to her chest and the house. He nodded his understanding and she duck walked away, sticking close to the car's body.

"I heard about Damon's death. I'm so sorry," he told her.

She inhaled shakily. "I went to see him this morning. I don't know why he did that ... killed himself."

"You were very close, weren't you?" he asked gently.

"We used to be. When I was a little girl, I worshipped him, and he spoiled me. It used to drive my parents bonkers, how he'd give me anything I wanted. They told him he was ruining me for men." She laughed manically.

Bodhi and Tory exchanged a look. Hope's laughter

was shrill and almost hysterical. She was teetering on the edge of a breakdown.

"You said you used to be close. What happened to make you grow apart?"

He watched the detectives take up positions on opposite sides of the front door with their weapons drawn.

"He left. When I was thirteen, he joined the Army. He came back whenever he got leave, but it wasn't the same. He wasn't around when I needed him."

"That must've been tough."

"I guess. But it taught me to look out for myself and go after what I wanted instead of waiting for someone to give it to me."

Up on the porch, Detective Gilbert raised a gloved hand and flashed one finger, then two, and then three. As he pulled back his boot to kick in the door, Bodhi said, "Can you see to the end of the street?"

"Uh, why?"

"I thought I heard a siren but I don't see any vehicles."

He watched as she leaned out the second-story window, holding the gun in her right hand and the phone in her left, and craned her head to look around the bend in her street.

The door gave way, and the detectives sprinted inside.

"I don't see any lights," Hope told him.

In the background, he heard Detective Gilbert's deep voice shouting commands. An instant later, Detective Martin appeared in the window behind Hope. The detective used her weapon to chop down on Hope's wrist and the gun flew from her grip and fell, turning end over end in the air as it headed to the ground.

Instinctively, Bodhi covered his head with one arm and pushed Tory's head down with his other hand. But the gun hit the frozen earth with a thud and nothing more.

Inside, someone disconnected the telephone call from Hope's end. Bodhi dropped his phone on the seat and turned to Tory.

"You okay?"

She nodded.

They sat in silence and watched as Detective Gilbert and Detective Martin escorted a handcuffed Hope Noor through the broken-down front door. As they passed by Tory's SUV, Detective Gilbert touched two fingers to his forehead and nodded to Bodhi.

CHAPTER THIRTY-FIVE

Four days later

The previous week's snow had melted into a gray slush, helped along by the cold rain that had been falling for the past day and a half. Bodhi turned up his collar and shivered. The weather was fitting for a funeral. Or more accurately, an interment of ashes.

Penny had handled the arrangements after it became clear that Hope Noor, who'd been taken to the psychiatric hospital for evaluation after her arrest, had no intentions of doing so. Damon Tenley had been cremated. His remains were placed in a basic, simple urn. Saul, who had a good relationship with the cemetery director, convinced him to bury Damon's remains in Frank and Lisa Kessler's family plot, between the only parents Damon had ever known.

And now, Penny, Bodhi, and Saul huddled together under a black canopy to bear witness to the burial of the urn.

"Does anyone want to say a few words?" the cemetery worker asked.

Saul and Penny shook their heads.

Bodhi spoke, "'The world is afflicted by death and decay. But the wise do not grieve, having realized the nature of the world.' The Buddha said this in the *Sutta Nipata*."

Saul turned to him as the man lowered the urn into the ground. "Really? That's kind of grim, don't you think?"

"Damon Tenley lived. He loved the girl whom he thought of as a sister. He served his country. And he killed an innocent woman as she lay sleeping in her bed. Then, unable or unwilling, to help his sister escape justice for her crimes, he took his own life. If the twisted path his life took doesn't convince you that the Buddha's correct about the nature of the world, I don't know what will."

They lapsed into silence while the man piled wet earth over the urn.

After a moment, Penny said, "Thanks for coming. I expected to be here alone, to tell you the truth."

"Of course," Saul answered. He offered the public defender his arm to navigate the slick grass as they walked to their cars.

Bodhi took a last look at the fresh earth that now marked Damon Tenley's final resting place and trailed Penny and Saul to the parking pad.

"Do you guys want to get a drink?" Penny asked.

"I can't," Bodhi said. "In fact, I was sort of hoping I could bum a ride to the airport from one of you."

"Headed back to Iowa?" Saul asked.

"It's still Illinois."

"Same difference."

"Really not. And yes. My tenant returned from her business trip this morning, so she doesn't need a house sitter. I thought I'd get away for a few days."

"Just a few?"

Bodhi shrugged. "We'll see where my path leads."

Penny extended her hand. "I'm going to run, then. I've blocked off my afternoon, so if nobody wants to raise a glass to a dead murderer, I'll see if I can't squeeze in a visit to my optometrist. Safe travels."

They shook hands all around, and she hopped into

her car. Bodhi and Saul stood side by side and watched her pull out of the cemetery.

"Do you think Meghan will charge Hope?" Bodhi asked.

Saul sucked air through his teeth. "I'm not sure. She's hyper-concerned about her win percentage, and she knows Hope would make a sympathetic defendant. If she pulled a jury of men, I'm not convinced she wouldn't walk—despite being responsible for two deaths."

Bodhi twisted his neck to look back at the plot of land where Damon Tenley's remains were buried. "Three," he corrected his friend.

"Three," Saul agreed. "If nothing else, she's off the streets. Detective Gilbert told me Roland promised to move to have her committed even if she doesn't stand trial, whether Meghan likes it or not."

"That's something."

"It is." Saul clapped his gloved hand on Bodhi's shoulder. "Come on. Let's get you to the airport so you can be on your way to Indiana."

"Illinois."

"Same difference."

Bodhi smiled and said nothing.

AUTHOR'S NOTE

As always, Bodhi provided a buffet of tasty research topics for me to dig into!

I was teaching a homeschool writing class centered on Greek myths when I read about the mythological Chimera, which made me curious about what other cultures had mythology about a hybrid beast. (Turns out, it's most of them.)

Shortly after that, I read about genetic chimerism issues in family law cases and as a (failed) defense in a cycling doping case as part of a roundup of odd legal decisions. (Yes, this is the sort of thing a recovering lawyer reads for fun!) From there, I was off to the races researching vanishing twin syndrome, transplant-induced chimerism, and fetomaternal microchimerism.

From there, I started devouring law review articles,

books, and medical journal studies, and my plot developed. Â Most of this source material is pretty dense, but you might enjoy reading a handful of interesting and well-written articles about the use (and misuse) of forensic DNA evidence here and here.

If you find the topic as fascinating as I do, I recommend this book, Inside the Cell: the Darkside of Forensic DNA.

One final note, when Bodhi travels to Carlisle, Pennsylvania, to borrow the rapid DNA machine, he's actually in my neck of the woods! Cumberland County really was an early adopter of the technology, as mentioned here.

The machine really is housed in the historic county jail, and I think of it almost every time I walk past the building while my kids are in their nearby martial arts class.

THANK YOU!

Thanks for reading *Twisted Path!* Bodhi will be back in another adventure soon. While you wait, you can always find an up-to-date list of the titles in this series, as well as my other books, on my website, www.melissafmiller.com

Sign up. To be the first to know when I have a new release, sign up for my email newsletter. Prefer text alerts? Text BOOKS to 636-303-1088 to receive new release alerts and updates. Subscribers receive new release alerts, notices of sales and other book news, goodies, and exclusive subscriber bonuses.

Keep reading. Check out the first book in one (or all) of my other three series:

Irreparable Harm (Sasha McCandless Legal Thriller No. 1):

Sasha's a five-foot nothing attorney who's trained in

Krav Maga. She's smart, funny, and utterly fearless. More than one million readers agree: you wouldn't want to face off against her in court ... or in a dark alley.

Critical Vulnerability (Aroostine Higgins Thriller No. 1):

Aroostine relies on her Native American traditions and her legal training to right wrongs and dispense justice. She's charmingly relentless, always dots her *i*'s and crosses her *t*'s, and is an expert tracker.

Rosemary's Gravy (We Sisters Three Humorous Romantic Mystery No. 1):

Rosemary, Sage, and Thyme are three twenty-something sisters searching for career success and love. Somehow, though, they keep finding murder and mayhem ... and love.

Share it. If you liked this book, please lend your copy to a friend who might enjoy it.

Review it. Please consider posting a short review. Honest reader reviews help others decide whether they'll enjoy a book.

ACKNOWLEDGMENTS

As always, I want to thank everyone involved in bringing this book to life, including my fantastic design team and each of my fabulous editors and proofreaders. Any errors that remain are my fault, and my fault alone.

Special thanks to David, for biting his tongue when this book dragged on past its deadline, and to Wendy Dorfman for stepping up to help me polish it to a shine.